A VIRGIN
FOR THE
BACHELOR
Billionaire

ROSE M. COOPER

OSHUN
PUBLICATIONS
oshunpublications.com

A Virgin for the Bachelor Billionaire © by Rose M. Cooper

Published by Oshun Publications
9 Old Kings Road STE. 123 #1038
Palm Coast, FL 32137
www.oshunpublications.com

Disclaimer
This is a work of fiction. Names, characters, places, and incidents either are the product of the author's imagination or are used fictitiously. Any resemblance to actual persons, living or dead, events, or locales is entirely coincidental.

Book design by Oliviaprodesign
www.fiverr.com/oliviaprodesign

ISBN 978-1-956319-89-7 (Paperback)
ISBN 978-1-956319-90-3 (Hardback)
ISBN 978-1-956319-88-0 (eBook)

Also by Rose M. Cooper

AVAILABLE IN AUDIO!

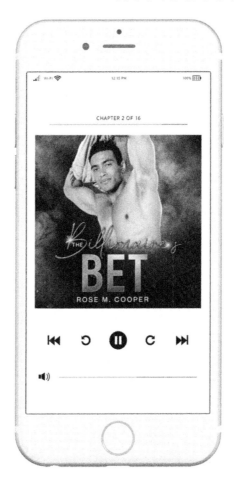

GET YOUR GENRE FIX TODAY! JOIN MY NEWSLETTER FOR MY RECOMMENDATIONS AND UPDATES!

ROSEMAECOOPER.COM

CHAPTER 1
Desperation

Amina Bethune sat in the lobby of Grandview Community Care and Hospice. Her foot tapped impatiently against the sterile white flooring. The clock on the wall ticked far louder than it should have, and the chatter of the nurses at the reception desk was a dull drone in her ear. No matter how often she had been here, it always set her on edge. While it also cared for many chronically ill patients, the fact that it was attached to a hospice was not lost on her. It was a near-constant reminder that her sister Serena's life was on a rickety seesaw. It didn't help her anxiety that the doctor asked to speak to her privately before she went to her sister's room.

She ran her hands through her thick curls anxiously and fiddled with her glasses. Her sister, Serena, had been diagnosed with pulmonary hypertension. At first, it had just been affording her sister's medication. But then Serena started needing regular oxygen treatments and couldn't work anymore. Then she had to be monitored constantly by doctors while they tried everything they could think of. It had taken a toll on her over the past couple of years. Amina had to drop out of college to pay for her sister's medical bills and work full-time. Not that she could get a well-paying job without her college degree.

But none of that mattered to Amina. Serena was the only family she had. Their mother died when Amina and Serena were both very young, and their father passed away just as Amina finished high school. They were all that they had. And Amina would do anything to keep her family alive and thriving.

The doctor came out with a clipboard in hand and a grim expression. Amina would have stood up, but her legs felt like jelly.

"I'm not going to lie, Miss Bethune, your sister's condition is not improving," the doctor said. "If she has a prayer of getting better, she will need some intensive care. But even that is only going to buy her so much time. Her only hope of living beyond that is a complete heart-lung transfer." Amina felt like all the breath had been sucked from her body, and gravity was crushing her.

"But that costs so much money," Amina said, trembling. Even the charity hospice wasn't exactly a cheap deal. And to top that off, it would take time to find Serena a donor and get her to the top of the donor list. But even with that, a hospital wouldn't even consider the surgery if Amina couldn't prove they had it covered by health insurance. The only paltry insurance Amina could afford wouldn't even consider half of the medicine Serena needed to survive. Unless Amina consistently proved that her sister hadn't miraculously been cured.

"I understand your financial situation. You aren't the first family member here struggling with medical bills. Suppose care cannot be found... well, in that case, our hospice counselors are available to help you both make a decision," the doctor said before leaving her alone with her thoughts.

Sitting there moping about the situation wouldn't do her

any good. She came here to visit her sister, after all. Plastering a smile, she made her way to Serena's room. She took another moment to compose herself at the door before knocking enthusiastically.

"Hey there, Serena," she chirped as she entered. Her sister had a tiny room. It only had room for a bed, a small dresser, and a bathroom. Her face would mirror Amina's thick curls, dark skin, and all if it weren't for how sunken her face looked. She had permanent dark circles under her eyes. The oxygen mask on her face was foggy with every strained breath she took.

"I can't stay too long. I have a shift this morning," Amina said as she sat on the bed. "How are you feeling today?" It took every bit of strength she had to keep her voice cheerful. Serena was pale and wheezing slightly with each inhale, even with the oxygen mask on. But Serena also seemed melancholy, staring out her tiny window at the small flower garden outside. Right outside her window were foxgloves, her favorite flower.

"I think this might be the big one, Anna." Serena sighed. There was robustness to her face. A calm acceptance that always set Amina on edge. Whenever Serena took a turn, she often became quiet and reflective.

"Now, don't be like that." Amina cleared her throat. Serena looked at her, sadness echoing behind her tired and sick eyes.

"What if it is, though? What if this time I actually die?" Serena asked. Amina opened and closed her mouth as she couldn't find the words. Serena couldn't die. Her sister was the only family she had left. She had put everything into caring for her sister and her health. If she were to die, Amina didn't know what she would do.

Amina shook her head. She couldn't think like that. She wouldn't let Serena die without a fight. But if she was going to do that, she had to focus on the positives. Amina would get the money for her sister to have her transplant. No matter what, Serena would live.

"You aren't going to die," she said, with more force than she intended. She placed a hand on Serena's knee and repeated herself more gently. Serena didn't look convinced, but she forced a smile for Amina's sake.

"You're right. I'm being morose again," Serena said. Amina pulled out a book she had taken from the library for Serena. Reading was one of the few activities left that Serena had the energy for.

"As promised, the latest and greatest on the fiction shelves." She placed the novel on the bedside table.

"You're too good to me, Amina," Serena said as she gently picked up the book. Many people would say Amina had the right to feel resentful of her situation. But Amina never felt even a fragment of bitterness. The way she saw it, it was only natural that she looked after her sister. After all, they were all they had for family. And as far as Amina was concerned, you always looked out for the family.

But the cost of her care was no joke. Amina was working like a dog at a cafe, just trying to scrape by with her paycheck and tips. By the time she had looked after Serena's cost of care, she barely had anything left for herself. Even paying her rent was a struggle, not that her apartment was the nicest. It was more like a closet than a room.

An alarm on Amina's phone went off. She resisted the urge to sigh. Back to the grind again.

"I should go. Let you get your rest. I'll be back tomorrow after work, ok?" she said. Serena nodded. Amina couldn't help but feel a twist in her stomach as she left the hospice. Serena isn't going to die. Not as long as I have anything to say about it.

A Cuppa Love greeted her with its usual cheerful chime as Amina opened the door. She scanned for Maren, hoping the elderly owner would be in so she could ask to work more shifts. But as she dipped into the back, Maren was nowhere to be seen. She probably still isn't feeling well. Realistically, Maren should have retired ages ago, but she insisted she would work at A Cuppa Love till the day she died.

It looks like I'll have to call her later.

"Hi, Piper," she called out to her coworker as she scrambled to get her apron on. Piper examined a cuticle between customers and responded with a noncommittal "hey." It suited Amina just fine. She just wanted to get into the rhythm of her work and forget all about everything.

Once upon a time, Amina had aspirations outside of the minimum wage, but she had to admit that making coffee every day wasn't the worst way to earn a living. Sure, you had the early-morning zombies and the Karens. Still, there was something rhythmic and relaxing about making different drinks. The aroma of coffee simultaneously perked her up and calmed her.

But today, she was having difficulty getting into the swing of things. The whole time she was prepping Lattes, Macchiatos, and Americanos, all that went through her mind were numbers. She was trying to calculate how many hours she would work to pay for her sister's transplant surgery. But no matter how much she worked it out in her head, she realized there weren't enough hours in a day to make what she needed on minimum wage. Even with her tips, she could barely scratch a quarter of the cost.

While doing her calculations, she noticed one of her regulars get in line. He was this cute guy named Kieran who had been coming there for a couple of weeks. She attempted a smile, but as she did, she almost dropped the tray of pastries she was replacing. She cursed under her breath. Her head was just not in the game today. Apparently, she wasn't the only one who noticed.

"You doing alright there, sweetie?" Piper asked. Amina always hated how Piper called her "sweetie", but she was the closest thing Amina had to a confidant. She was at least aware of Serena's health issues.

"Not really. Serena is getting worse. She needs a transplant as soon as possible if we want the outlook to improve. But I don't know how I'm going to make that kind of money," Amina said as her brows knitted tightly in worry. So much for trying not to think about it. She thought getting it off her chest would make her feel better since ignoring it was clearly doing nothing, but the knot in her chest only clenched harder.

Piper looked at her quizzically for a moment. Whatever Amina thought she would say next, she was unprepared for the words that came out of her coworker's mouth.

"Are you a virgin by any chance?" Piper asked. The question was so sudden that Amina almost dropped the saucer she had just grabbed.

"Excuse me?" Amina said incredulously. While it was confirmed that she was still a virgin, it wasn't exactly like she was broadcasting that. It was nothing she was ashamed of. It was hard to date when she was always working. But it wasn't quite workplace-appropriate enough to talk about at the cafe.

"Oh, you totally are," Piper cackled. Amina felt her whole face turn red.

"Hey, don't sweat it. It's perfect. Look, just hear me out. There's this super exclusive club. You have to be born with a million dollars in your crib exclusive. Anyways, these rich guys in the club are into some really kinky shit. I bet if you tried to auction off your virginity at one of their soirees, they'd pay more than you need to cover Serena's hospital bills," Piper explained.

"Are you crazy? How do you even know about this?"

Amina asked. After all, if Piper was telling the truth, it wasn't exactly something just anybody would have common knowledge about.

"My cousin got into a bit of a rough spot with money. I mean, she was pole dancing to pay her rent. One night, one of the guys gave her this card, and one thing led to another." It was undoubtedly one of the most incredulous stories Amina had ever heard in her entire life. Losing her virginity shouldn't be done in such a blasé manner, as if it didn't mean anything. She couldn't imagine having that moment with someone for whom she at least didn't feel something. While she wasn't under the illusion that it had to be the most romantic experience of her life, Amina knew she wanted more to it than that.

But she would be a fool not to admit that she was desperate for money. This might just be her only shot. And she would get the money quickly. In the grand scheme of Serena's life, Amina's virginity meant very little.

CHAPTER 2
The Billionaire Bachelor

To say that Kieran Holland liked mornings wouldn't have been entirely truthful. Usually, each morning came with the dreaded onslaught of emails and phone calls about one or more of his factories. Life got pretty busy when you were the founder and CEO of one of North America's leading men's formal wear companies.

However, recently he was finding mornings to be more tolerable. And it all had to do with a cute barista at a cafe. A few weeks ago, Kieran desperately needed a heavy dose of caffeine. So, on a whim, he pulled into a cafe called A Cuppa Love. That was when he met Amina for the first time.

She was unmistakably beautiful. Her dark skin was clear, and she always had a warm, bright smile that cheerfully greeted everyone. Her thick-rimmed glasses added a touch of character to her face that drew Kieran to look at her eyes more often than he would have liked. But her most striking feature had to be her hair. Her thick, natural curls framed her face almost like a halo. He met many women with natural hair that thick, but there was just something about hers that just drew him even further in. She had him hooked when he watched her make his first Cortado. She was magnetic in everything she did. Kieran couldn't quite put his finger on it, but he could never look away as she worked.

After that, coming into A Cuppa Love quickly became a morning habit. He would come in every morning on his way to work and order the same thing. An Americano doesn't sound like anything unique or distinct. But there was just something remarkable about the way she made hers. He couldn't explain it, no matter how slowly he savored it to try to figure it out.

That morning was no different than any other morning in the past couple of weeks. Kieran got in his car and made his usual stop at A Cuppa Love. As usual, Amina was running around like a chicken with her head cut off for the morning rush. However, he noticed something odd about her today. She usually got into this kind of rhythm when she was working. It amazed him that she never looked bored doing something as menial as making coffee a million times a day. This time, however, her eyebrows were knitted together—a distinct difference between her friendly and easygoing personality. If he had to hazard a guess, he would say she was very worried about something

Kieran waited in line, still unable to tear his eyes away from Amina. He wondered if he just had the opportunity to sleep with her, he'd be able to get her out of his head. However, he didn't want to ruin his little morning routine until he gauged if she was also attracted to him. He didn't exactly want to scare her. He knew very little of her, but he knew that she was a genuine and kind person. Since he had been coming here, he had seen her give free treats and coffee to the homeless that lingered outside the cafe.

Asking someone like that to sleep with you just for the sake of it came with a lot on the line. For one thing, there was an excellent chance she would say no. The other problem would be that if he did sleep with her just for the hell of it without laying down that he wasn't looking for a relationship, there was a very good chance of miscommunication leading to hurt feelings.

She didn't really deserve that. Not from him. Genuinely kind people are such a commodity these days. No matter what people said, most were out to get something from somebody else. He had enough business and life experience to know that it was a cutthroat world. But Amina was different. She smiled at everyone and always did her best to help people. Kieran could tell many regulars adored being served by her, and he could see why.

He tuned into the conversation that Amina was having with her coworker when he noticed the serious expression on Amina's face. Judging by how her brow was furled and how she kept biting the inside of her cheek, it was obvious she was stressed about something.

"I just don't know how I'm going to make that kind of money," Amina said to her coworker. She immediately grabbed Kieran's attention. He knew that Amina likely earned the minimum wage plus whatever pitiful pittance was left behind in the tip jar. But he had never heard her complain about money before today.

"Are you a virgin?" her coworker responded. Then she proceeded to tell Amina about the craziest idea.

The fact that she would even seem to entertain the idea of selling her virginity was nothing short of appalling. Just how desperate was she? Was she in some kind of trouble?

He finally got up to the counter and was greeted by Amina's warm smile. However, the contrast between the conversation and her customer service attitude was so stark that it made his stomach churn.

"Good morning, Kieran. Cortado to go as usual?" she asked in her overcompensatingly sweet voice.

"Actually, I think I'll have it in-house today," he said. Amina blinked, confused for a moment, but said nothing. Typically, Kieran took his coffee to go. He often worried that if he hung around the cafe for too long, Amina would not only get suspicious of his attraction to her but might also consider him a stalker. It was a simple boundary meant to keep him in check. To make sure that he didn't cross a line and scare Amina off.

But after hearing that unpleasant conversation, he felt he needed to know more. Just what exactly had Amina gotten herself entangled in? He needed to ask her about it. If she was involved with something sketchy, there had to be something he could do about it. At the very least, he could help with whatever she needed the money for. It's not like he was pinching pennies and saving them for a rainy day.

Amina wasn't the type who would take money as a gesture of goodwill, though. Plus, he ran the risk of again seeming like a complete creep and insulting her. Sure, he had experience with people who would have groveled for a fraction of his money. Still, he also knew plenty of people were far too proud for a handout, regardless of whether or not they actually needed it.

How will I get her to agree to take the money and keep her away from that horrible club? I—

His phone buzzed suddenly. He glanced down and saw a text from his sister, Scout. He barely had to look at the text to know what she wanted to ask him.

Scout: *Hey, you never said if you were bringing a plus one to the wedding.*

He resisted the urge to roll his eyes. He thought that by now, Scout would realize that the dating thing wasn't his scene. As much as he was desperately attracted to Amina, he wasn't exactly looking to get too heavily involved with her. Relationships were complicated and could be messy. It circled back to the whole, risking people getting hurt when things went south.

But right as Amina was finishing making his Cortado at the counter, he looked down at his text message, and the idea formed from a dull whisper to an outright scheme. There was a way he could help Amina.

Kieran: *Actually, put me down for a plus one. I'm bringing a date.*

CHAPTER 3
Strike a Deal

Amina couldn't help but stare at Kieran. It was rather strange to her that he was drinking his coffee in the cafe. He had such a routine. She would have made his Cortado ahead of him showing up if she wasn't so busy with other people's orders all the time. She took notice of the regulars who came in, and Kieran had been coming in for a few solid weeks. She chalked it up to the fact that she made dang good coffee. And she had to admit, she liked seeing him. He always tipped really well, but beyond that, he was nice to her. And she had to admit he was quite attractive as well.

Kieran had tight, dark curls that were cut close to his scalp, and he had a very well-manicured strap of facial hair lining the edges of his face. Overall, he looked quite dashing and distinguished. She figured he probably had an excellent job based on how expensive his clothes looked. No matter what, he always came into A Cuppa Love in a clearly custom-tailored suit. Despite this, however, he never looked down on her while she was serving him. That was a rarity with the corporate types who sometimes stopped in. They thought that because they were blessed with an education and a good job, they were better than any barista. Amina was used to dealing with those types. She would just kill them with kindness and a warm smile.

She wondered if those billionaires at that club Piper talked about would be as nice as Kieran often was to her. The thought of what she would have to do for whoever bid the highest on her made her stomach acid crawl painfully up her esophagus. She shook her head.

She walked towards Kieran's table and noticed that he looked at her oddly. Typically, he was pretty friendly with her, often asking how her day was going—that sort of thing. But now, something was different. He was staring at her with a kind of interest that was, in all honesty, a little intense. She couldn't make heads or tails of it. But it made her weirdly uncomfortable. It made her think that she would have to stand on a stage wearing God knows what and have a bunch of men bid. The more she thought about it, the more her anxiety grew. But still, she had a job to do. She tightened her grip on the rim of the saucer. She just had to get through the day and get the information she needed from Piper after hours. She wanted to get it over with sooner rather than later.

"Nice to see you're taking time to enjoy your coffee today," Amina said, smiling at him. In part, she was making a genuine attempt at polite conversation. However, she would be lying if she said she wasn't trying to distract herself from her situation. *The more I think about it, the more likely I will change my mind.* She couldn't afford to let her conviction waver for even a millisecond. Amina was going to do this. It was the only way.

"Thank you, Amina," he said, taking a sip of his drink. He closed his eyes and took a long and appreciative sip. It always made Amina feel better when she saw people enjoying her coffee. It was like she was making their day just a bit better with something warm and delicious. He set his saucer down and smiled at her.

"Delicious as always," he said. He was polite as usual, but still, Amina couldn't shake the sense that he wanted to say something to her. She had no idea what he could want to talk about aside from their usual pleasantries. He was very consistent. Get in, say hello, order a coffee, and leave. He was utterly throwing Amina for a loop today.

"Just let me know if you need anything," Amina said, lamely trying to excuse herself.

"Before you go, I wanted to ask you something," Kieran said, leaning forward slightly. Amina blinked. She wondered if he was going to try to ask her out. She had been asked out by men at the cafe before but had always turned them down politely. It was a shame that she might have to do the same to Kieran because she genuinely thought he was friendly and cute. But how on earth could she explain to a guy, "Hey, I'd like to grab a drink sometime, but I'm about to sell my freaking virginity for fast cash." Yeah, there was no universe in which that would go well.

Whatever Amina had been expecting Kieran to say, she couldn't have prepared for the words that came out of his mouth.

"I couldn't help but overhear your conversation at the counter," Kieran said.

"I'm sorry?" she said, holding the tray closer to her body. Amina felt her heart leap into her throat. She hoped he wasn't talking about what she thought he was talking about. Because if he was, she would undoubtedly die right then and there in the middle of the cafe. Kieran glanced around as if he was making sure no one was listening. Then, when he was certain no one was, he leaned closer to Amina.

"I heard your conversation about needing money... and what you're willing to do to acquire it," he continued. Oh

God. Curse Piper and her lack of volume control. If Amina could have crawled into a hole and died, she would have dug it herself. Instead, her face was aflame, and she wanted to run.

"Um... I can explain," she said, fumbling. Amina was trying to find an excuse, but honestly, none came to mind. She was tempted to stop the conversation and return to the counter, but somehow she couldn't move her feet. She glanced back at the counter. The rush was beginning to die, so Piper paid more attention to her phone between customers than she was to the painfully awkward situation Amina found herself in. *Thanks, Piper. I really appreciate this.*

"I know that you were talking to your coworker about needing money. And to be quite frank, I find her 'suggestion' laughably crude," he said. Oh shit. He had heard their conversation, after all.

"I have a proposal that I think will benefit you a lot more and help you avoid sacrificing so much," Kieran continued, taking another sip of his coffee. Oh God. Was she about to suggest something akin to what she and Piper had discussed? Instead of auctioning it off, would he convince her to give him her virginity for money? Her knees wobbled, and she put a hand on the other chair to steady herself. Despite how desperate she was, actually being in the situation made her feel more frightened than she had ever felt in her entire life. Every muscle in her body was poised to run, yet she was still frozen.

"Just... just wait a second. I don't know what you think you heard, but I can assure you—" Kieran held up a hand to cut her off.

"I promise that there is nothing unsavory about my offer. I won't be asking you to do anything like what those bastards at a club like that will ask of you," he said. Amina searched his face to see if there was even a hint of deception in his dark brown eyes. They remained unwavering and focused on her, no matter how hard she looked. When she suddenly realized it probably looked like she was staring at him, she ducked her head down. Could this get any more humiliating?

"What would I have to do then?" she whispered. This is crazy. No, not crazy. This was full-on insane. For all she knew, he could be asking her to do something far worse than lose her virginity. Sure, he seemed nice enough, but what kind of guy would offer a woman he barely knew a million dollars? He had to be scheming something. There was no way anyone could be that generous out of the goodness of their hearts. For all she knew, he could be trying to sex-traffic her or make her launder money for him or do something so terrible she couldn't even fathom it right now.

But if it wasn't too illegal, it had to be much better than selling her body to some sleaze ball, sipping a martini, and glowering over her naked body. She shuddered at the very image.

"All I ask is that you attend my sister's wedding with me as my date. Do that, and I'll gladly give you a million dollars. Upon completing this task, you will be transferred your money, and I will take care of any monitoring of your account as a result," Kieran offered. He leaned back again in his chair and folded his arms, clearly waiting to see Amina's reaction.

If she was stunned before, she was flabbergasted now. Was that seriously all? Was he offering to pay her a million freaking dollars to have her pretend to be his girlfriend just for a weekend? It sounded more like something out of a romance comedy movie than some sinister scheme.

She shook her head. Maybe he wanted her to think this whole thing was ridiculous. Get her to let her guard down and swoop in when she was least expecting it.

"Why on earth would you offer something like that? I mean, what exactly are you hoping to get out of this?" Amina blurted out when she managed to find her voice again.

"Let's just say it will help my family get off my back about my dating life. They are getting insistent that I find a nice girl like you and settle down," he explained.

"Ok. But why offer to pay me? Especially that much?" There was no chance Kieran couldn't find a date if he was actively trying to. If he was that handsome and rich enough that he could just throw a million dollars away on a whim, there had to be someone out there who would go with him to a freaking wedding for free. There had to be some kind of catch.

"It's simple. You need the money. I need a date. Both of us win. Besides, I can't stand the idea of some sleazeball putting their mitts on someone of your caliber," he said. Amina's cheeks reddened. Maybe he was just trying to flatter her, but she couldn't help but feel slightly complimented.

There was no telling whether or not he would keep his word or if he was secretly up to something incredibly sketchy or illegal. But honestly, what choice did Amina have? Considering the options were to sell her body or attend a wedding and pretend to be this stranger's girlfriend, it's not like she could afford to be picky.

"Alright," Amina said. "First, some ground rules. Sex is completely and utterly off the table, understood?" Kieran held up his hands in surrender and nodded.

"Naturally," he agreed, though Amina didn't miss the ghost of a smirk on his lips. It would be very tempting to smack him for that if she weren't at work.

"Second, you never speak of it again after this is through. If you enter the cafe, our interactions will be limited to the usual customer-employee exchange," she continued. Kieran nodded thoughtfully.

"Those are reasonable terms. So do we have a deal?" Kieran asked.

Amina sighed, extending her hand. "Deal." He shook her

hand firmly, and Amina noted his warm hand. She hoped she hadn't made a proverbial deal with the devil.

"What exactly makes you so desperate for money, by the way?" Kieran asked.

"With all due respect, that isn't really any of your business, is it?" Amina's tone was more snappish than she intended. Kieran's eyebrows shot up at her tone, but he nodded and didn't press her. The last thing Amina wanted was for him to know about her family. If he was really up to something shifty —well, this way, she was the only one who would get hurt. The more she kept Serena out of this, the better.

"Alright. We'd have to get in touch about the details when it's getting closer to the date. I'll give you my number," he said, pulling a pen out of his jacket pocket and writing on the paper napkin. Amina glanced down and noticed how neat and precise his handwriting was. He looked up at her expectantly.

"I need your number too," he said. Adrenaline coursed through Amina's veins. This was really happening. She wrote her number on the notepad, took orders, and handed it to him.

"Alright. I will be in touch soon, Amina," he said, getting up from the table and walking out the door as quickly as he had come in.

Amina made her way back to the counter robotically. She still couldn't fully believe that had even happened.

"Are you ok? Did that guy say anything weird to you?" Piper asked, shifting her gaze over to Kieran who neatly folded his napkin on his saucer before glancing back at Amina. Her cheeks flushed again, and she tore her eyes back to Piper.

"Yeah, everything is fine," she said. Piper frowned, clearly unconvinced, but did not push the issue—a rare occurrence for her. Amina took the next customer's order and tried hard not to think about deal she had just agreed to.

CHAPTER 4
Beauty and Boutiques

Kieran couldn't believe what he had gotten himself into. This had to be possibly the most brazen and ridiculous idea he had ever come up with. Not because of the money. He had more disposable income than he honestly knew what to do with on an average day. The problem was how he had roped himself into making Amina his date. Even standing next to Amina was going to be a test of willpower.

It didn't help that when he mentioned her to his sister, he may have made it sound like Amina and he had been going out for some time. They'd never believe he would bother bringing some casual fling to the wedding. Kieran wasn't the type to really bring girls home, so he knew that to get the family on board, he had to make it sound like they were very serious.

As a result, he needed to get her ready for the weekend. And that, unfortunately, meant they would need to make a few tweaks.

But now she was making things difficult by running late.

Kieran waited outside the boutique impatiently. He told Amina they had to prepare her for the big day. Even though Amina looked beautiful in torn jeans and a coffee-stained T-shirt, that wouldn't cut it for the wedding. Not by a long shot. So he wanted to prepare her for what to expect. Besides, no one in his family would believe that he would bring a date and not spring for a dress on her if she didn't have one of her own.

"I'm sorry I'm late," Amina said, panting heavily as she adjusted the strap of her purse on her shoulder. He'd say it sounded like she had been rushing to get here if he didn't know better. But he could tell by the shifting of her eyes that she was incredibly nervous.

"Why did you want to meet outside of a boutique exactly?" she asked once she had caught her breath.

"You'll need something to wear for the wedding," he said as if it was the most obvious thing in the world. Amina's eyes widened.

"Are you insane? I can't afford anything in there!" she said, tilting her head towards the store.

"I'll take care of it, and don't worry, it won't come off your payout for the wedding," he said, gesturing to her. He held the door open for her, but she stayed rooted to the spot.

"Is any of this really necessary? I do own a dress, you know," Amina said, folding her arms over her chest. While Kieran didn't doubt that she owned a semi-decent dress, he knew she wasn't prepared for how formal Scout's wedding would be. A Holland spares no expense on the things that matter. His grandmother had drilled that into his head for years. If it meant Scout was happy, their grandmother would have given her the moon as a wedding present if possible.

"Trust me. You'll feel a lot less awkward if my family asks a lot fewer questions about you that you may not want to answer," he insisted. She hesitated briefly before entering the shop without making eye contact with Kieran. Before they got within three feet of the shop, a shrill and excited voice echoed across the room.

"Kieran Holland! It's been ages," Bristol said with a wide smile. Bristol was Scout's stylist.

"And this must be the lovely Amina I have heard so much about," she said as she circled Amina. Amina's shoulders stiffened a bit, confused at what Bristol was doing. Not that Kieran could have told her. Bristol was her own breed of interesting. She was good at her job, but he couldn't see how Scout could gab with her for hours. Then again, what else were you supposed to do when Bristol had you in her chair for up to four hours?

"I must say, Kieran, darling, you're lucky I adore you and Scout. Do you have any idea how busy I am with the wedding?" Bristol gushed.

"And we appreciate you for it."

"Umm, Kieran, this feels a little more... intense than dress shopping," Amina said, her eyes roving around the boutique. Her pupils widened when she saw the salon chair and hair-washing sink in the corner. Bristol liked covering all the bases for her clients, which was precisely what Kieran needed.

"I know. Just go with me on this, alright?"

"Alright, I have the perfect selection of gowns for you to try, and—"

"I don't know about all this. It's just a bit... much," Amina said, blinking as she stared down at the rows and rows of cosmetics and designer dresses. Kieran couldn't even name a third of the stuff the stylist had laid out as she patiently waited for Amina to get on board with the makeover.

But Amina looked absolutely frightened. He needed her to relax. If she was this tense during the weekend, she would risk blowing their cover.

"I get that you might be feeling a bit overwhelmed right now, but trust me, this is important if we want this to work. You have no idea how badly I need to show up with a date. If I don't, they aren't going to get off my back for at least another three months. My sister will try to set me up with all her single bridesmaids the second the cake is cut," Kieran said. It was a bit of a half-truth. Yes, it was likely that his sisters would gripe about how he was still single. Then conspire to play match-maker as soon as Scout and her fiancé sign the marriage license. But in truth, he didn't need Amina to be his date. It was more of a perk, so to speak. He got to help and keep her from debasing her dignity. He got the pleasure of being left in relative peace throughout the wedding. And in a way, he got to interact with her more outside of A Cuppa Love.

"Hmm... now what to do about the hair?" Bristol mused to herself, eyeballing Amina's thick curls. "Perhaps we could get more versatility if we silk-press it."

"I am not silk pressing my hair," Amina insisted firmly. It was as if any anxiety she was feeling had suddenly dissipated. A ghost of a smile tugged at Kieran's lips. He was glad Amina was firm about her hair. There was just something special about her thick, vibrant curls that fascinated him. He had met many girls who loved their curls, preferred their hair straight, and had never given much thought to their preferences. But when it came to Amina, he couldn't help but love how proud she was of her best feature.

"You heard her. No silk pressing." Kieran couldn't help but feel a sense of pride. He always thought her natural curls suited her. Bristol pursed her lips but didn't argue with him.

"First, we will start with the outfit. Then we'll match the makeup to suit it. We'll do a simple yet classic look. Something that will be easy for you to replicate on the weekend. I won't be able to help you. I need to get Scout and her entourage ready," Bristol said. She grabbed an armful of gown bags and sauntered towards the dressing room area.

"I wish I shared some of her enthusiasm," Amina said with an uncomfortable giggle.

"Trust me, you're in good hands with Bristol," he promised, placing a hand on her shoulder. He had meant for it to be a friendly gesture, but he was surprised at how warm she felt to the touch. He looked down at her and realized she was staring at him. Kieran tried to pull away but found he couldn't. He was getting lost in those warm, beautiful eyes. Completely fixated and entranced.

There was this weird magnetic energy that seemed to keep drawing Kieran closer and closer to Amina. Their faces were uncomfortably close, and he could have sworn he felt his breath catch in his throat. He wanted so badly to kiss her. He was surprised that Amina appeared to be leaning closer to him. Was that her giving some kind of signal? Did she also want to kiss him?

The cheerful chime on the boutique's doors immediately broke the tension. Kieran and Amina pulled away from each other as if suddenly shocked awake by a splash of cold water.

Kieran pulled away from Amina, feeling uncharacteristically sheepish. He wasn't usually like this when he had the opportunity to get to know a woman like this. He was usually all charm. But being around Amina made him nervous. And as much as he liked her, he was not overly fond of being nervous.

Kieran still had his eyes glued to the jewelry display case as Bristol clapped her hands eagerly.

"Let's go, darling. I do have a lot to get through today." Bristol pulled Amina along with her. Kieran sighed. At least that awkward moment was over.

If Kieran hadn't deliberately turned his attention to the jewelry display, he would have realized that he recognized the woman who walked into the boutique. Standing at the entrance was Raina, the best friend of Kieran's ex-girlfriend, Nyra. He would have also noticed Raina spotting him and Amina together in the shop and slyly taking a picture of the two to send to Nyra with a malicious grin.

CHAPTER 5
The Hollands

Amina had to admit that Kieran had been good with his word so far. He had already sent her half of the money, which was already more than enough. She was able to get Serena placed at Woodland Medical Hospital. Due to her condition, the transplant committee was looking at putting her at the top of the list, which made Amina almost burst into tears of relief. She had done it; her sister would live.

But the ordeal was far from over. Amina briefly considered hiding somewhere Kieran wouldn't be able to find her in time for the wedding. But as quickly as the thought came, she dismissed it. On the one hand, she wasn't the kind of person to back out of a deal. On the other hand, she had no way of knowing if he would come after her if she suddenly disappeared.

So rather than run like a coward, she doubled down on her commitment. She stood on the curb, waiting outside the café, with a duffle bag slung over her shoulder. Amina had insisted on being picked up outside of A Cuppa Love. When Kieran asked her if she had any garment bags for the dress, she informed him that her only option for a bag was the ratty duffle bag she'd had since junior high. He had quickly arranged for her dress to be delivered to his family's home. She was surprised that it even held all the makeup she had been given by Bristol on top of her clothes.

She wondered what his family would be like as she stood waiting for him. It would undoubtedly be an interesting weekend if they were anything like Kieran. Kieran himself was a challenging read. Sure, everything he had done so far had been incredibly kind, but she still couldn't figure out his motivation. Indeed, he could have found someone he wouldn't have had to pay to be his date. After all, he was rich and good-looking. A lot of girls would probably tear each other limb from limb to spend an evening with him. So, the real question was: What had possibly possessed him to pick her for the task? No matter how hard Amina tried to figure out his motive, she always came up blank. Especially considering he had also paid for her to be styled for the whole event.

Still, it didn't mean she had fully trusted him just yet. In fact, she was waiting outside A Cuppa Love for him because the last thing she wanted was for him to find out where she lived. For the most part, it was to protect her safety. If he was suddenly going to turn into a scumbag, the last thing she needed was him showing up at her door at three in the morning, even if everything else went off without a hitch.

A sleek red car pulled up to the front of the cafe. Amina didn't know much about cars, but she knew that it probably cost at least her rent times ten. The window rolled down, and she was surprised to see Kieran in the car. She hadn't anticipated for him to pick her up.

"Morning," he said as Amina slid into the passenger seat. She gave him a nod in greeting, and Kieran's engine roared to life. Kieran's family had a home in Rose Creek, a town 30 minutes from Portland, which she had never honestly heard of until Kieran had mentioned it to her. Amina wondered what they should talk about for that length of time in such an enclosed space. Anything would be preferable to talk about whatever weird tension was happening back at Bristol's Boutique.

"So, I should probably brief you on a few things about my family. You know, the kind of stuff even a relatively new girlfriend would know," Kieran said. Amina could have sighed in relief. At least he had a plan, so they didn't have to sit there in awkward silence.

"Sure, lay it on me," she said. She turned slightly towards Kieran to show she was engaged and open to the conversation. The more she learned, the less likely she was to make an awkward mess of this whole thing.

"I was raised by my grandmother, Esme Holland. I have three sisters: Scout, Tori, and Joyce. Scout is the one getting married to Quincy," he said. Amina wasn't sure she would remember the names he threw at her. A curious part of her wanted to ask why his grandmother raised the four of them, but she got the sense that it was a very sensitive topic. After all, she knew what it was like to not grow up with a mom. Whatever reason Esme had for raising Kieran and his siblings was between them and none of her business.

"My grandmother can be pretty traditional, so keep that in mind. And my sisters can be a bit noisy and boisterous," he continued.

"They sound intimidating," she said nervously, giggling.

"I don't think you have to worry too much. They're very lovely people," he said. Kieran had a warm, soft smile on his face that reassured Amina. If he meant what he was saying, she could probably be alright.

"What about your family?" Kieran asked. Amina felt a wave of nerves. It made sense for him to tell her about his family. After all, they would spend a lot of time together over the weekend. But Amina's reluctance to share about her family would not budge. For now, she would say nothing or, at the very least, the bare minimum.

"Not as big as yours, but pretty normal. That's all," she said. It was enough to give him something to work with. After all, it might be weird to the rest of his family if he didn't at least know that much. But she wasn't going to give him any details about her sister's health. He didn't need to know something personal about her family like that. Thankfully, Kieran didn't try to push much out of her, even if his gaze on her was filled with burning curiosity.

The house was huge. House wasn't even the right word. His family's home was a freaking mansion. Amina had to fight the urge to gawk. Kieran was obviously rich if he could afford to give her a million dollars without blinking. But this confirmed that he was on a whole different level than her.

They pulled up to the front of the house. A gentleman in a smart jacket opened Amina's door for her, and she tried not to give away that she was so taken aback by everything. A butler came to let her out of the car. This is insane. Standing at the top of the steps were a short woman who looked to be in her late fifties and a young woman whose face nearly mirrored Kieran's—with her short, cropped curls and all.

"Kieran, my boy, it's been far too long since you've been home," the shorter woman said. She was wearing Kieran leaned down so that she could give him a warm squeeze. When they were done hugging, the lady turned to Amina and smiled at her.

"Welcome, my dear. I'm Kieran's grandmother. Please call me Esme. Consider our home your home for the weekend," she said. Amina couldn't believe how young his grandmother was. Her hair was just beginning to become speckled with gray.

"It's very nice to meet you," Amina said, trying very hard

to avoid looking nervous. Quickly glancing at Kieran, she caught him nodding at her reassuringly.

"And you must be the Amina we've heard about," the woman around Amina's age said. A glance at her hand showed a large topaz ring. This must have been the bride, Scout.

"Yep, that would be me," she said. Scout insisted on taking her bag, and Esme ushered them into the entryway. The inside was even more immaculate than the outside. Rich reds, browns, and mahogany furniture littered every surface of the house. There was so much space and a collection of expensive-looking antiques that Amina had to look at Kieran to avoid being overwhelmed.

"Please come into the parlor. We were just chatting and catching up," Esme said, taking Amina's arm. Amina was very quickly ushered into the parlor, as mentioned earlier. Esme's hand on her arm was warm and reassuring, and Amina couldn't help but relax.

She was very quickly greeted with resounding enthusiasm. Tori and Joyce hugged her as if she was already part of the family, and Scout introduced what looked like the rest of the whole wedding guests. Amina was pleasantly surprised. Upon seeing the mansion's size, she assumed that Kieran's family might be a bit uppity and snobbish. But they were so warm right from the get-go. It was welcome compared to her expectations, but it was a lot to take in all at once.

Kieran squeezed her hand. A slight tremor went through her, and she quickly glanced around the room. Thankfully, no one had noticed her odd reaction to his touch. It felt odd holding his hand, but simultaneously, she was surprised. His grip was warm and firm, and she found the tension in her shoulders evaporating the longer he held her hand.

A woman with a clipboard came into the parlor. She wore a sharp suit, and her blonde hair was pulled into such a tight bun that it almost defied the laws of physics.

"If I could have everyone's attention, please," she said in an authoritative tone. She dug out a sleek black pen and tapped it against the clipboard. Amina glanced at Kieran, who mouthed "wedding planner" at her.

"The happy couple has selected several activities leading up to the day of the ceremony. I have compiled an itinerary for each event, starting with some exciting couples' games. The first thing on the list is the couples' question games."

"Oh, this is perfect with Kieran bringing Amina," Tori said with a giggle as she leaned closer to her boyfriend, one of Quincy's friends and groomsmen. Amina felt her stomach drop. She didn't know nearly enough about Kieran to pull anything like this off. And he certainly didn't know anything about her either. They were going to be found out in a matter of milliseconds. She looked around the room but noticed Scout and Joyce had a playful glint in their eyes when they looked at Kieran and Amina—no chance of getting out of this one.

"Sure, sounds like fun," Amina said, her throat constricting. Maybe they will let us go last so I can get myself psyched and prepped for it?

But Amina still needed to find such luck. Kieran's sisters were eager to get to know their brother's new girlfriend.

"How does Amina take her coffee?" Scout asked, leaning forward curiously.

"Latte with a pump of vanilla and a pinch of cinnamon," Kieran said without missing a single beat. Amina blinked in surprise. Though she had to admit that was probably an easy question to answer. One of the few benefits of being a minimum-wage barista was unlimited free coffee. There was no doubt that Kieran had seen her making her everyday drink at some point.

"Amina, what is Kieran's favorite food?" Tori asked. Oh

crap, oh crap. He very seldom ever ordered any food at the cafe. How on earth was she supposed to answer that?

"Oh, that's a hard one. He doesn't seem to be the picky type," she laughed nervously.

"Well, that is true," Esme said. "Probably because I raised him that way."

Phew, that was a close one.

"Especially if it's spicy. That's why, I guess, if I had to pick, I'd say I like a good curry," Kieran said pointedly. Amina tried to avoid looking sheepish. Maybe she should have quizzed him in the car.

Throughout the game, Amina was surprised to find that Kieran knew much more about her than she had anticipated. He knew what music she liked to listen to, her favorite pastry, and her favorite flowers. She had no idea how he would have picked up on this. Amina managed to skate by with vague answers, but it seemed as natural to him as breathing.

"Where did Amina go to high school?" Joyce asked.

"Oh, come on, Joyce, that one wasn't fair. High school is like ancient history for adults," Scout said.

"I'll have to admit that one escapes me," Kieran said with an easy laugh. Amina wondered how he was able to do this. All of this came easily to them. Like they were waltzing, and he had a firm grip on her waist. He led her the way he wanted to impress everyone or where he wanted the conversation to go. Everyone else was too caught up in the dance to notice Amina fumble all over the place.

"I can tell that Nyra is going to be fuming tomorrow at the wedding," Joyce said with a grin. Kieran's eyes widened, and Amina felt him stiffen beside her.

"Scout, why on earth was Nyra invited?" Kieran asked.

"Now, now, I'm sure that Nyra has matured. If she's any problem at the wedding, I'd be more than happy to remind her of her place," Scout said with a shockingly vicious glint in her eyes.

"I'm sorry, but who is Nyra?" Amina asked.

"Just an ex. We didn't work out," Kieran explained. Amina sensed there was a bit more to the story than that. But it didn't feel like asking him about it in front of his entire family was appropriate. Besides, why would she care about Kieran having an ex-girlfriend show up at his sister's wedding? It's not like the two of them were actually a couple.

And yet she was shocked to find this odd flutter of insecurity in her chest.

"Well, then I suppose we should call it an evening," Esme said. Amina hadn't even noticed that it had gotten dark outside, let alone how late it was. Esme offered to show them to their rooms. As they walked, Kieran leaned down and whispered to her,

"That went well." She could tell he meant it, but she wasn't so reassured. She had no idea how she would pull this weekend off if she kept being so clumsy and uncertain when asked questions about Kieran.

She was entirely thrown for another loop when Esme revealed they would share a bedroom. So much for being traditional.

"Are you sure, Grandma? I mean, I wouldn't want you to think that we're doing anything improper," Kieran said. There was a slight bead of sweat on his forehead, though he kept his expression neutral.

"Oh, don't be silly. I'm not so much of a fuddy-duddy that I'm under the illusion that you two haven't shared a bed before," she said with a chuckle. Amina forced a grateful smile and took Kieran by the arm. He seemed surprised at her touch, much like she was at his earlier.

"Of course, thank you so much, Esme," she said warmly. She pulled Kieran into the room, and as soon as the door latched shut, she finally exhaled. She glanced around the room and saw it was larger than even her apartment—though apparently not large enough for two beds. But the large white bed did look rather big. Maybe they could manage to get through the night without any awkward touching.

"Relax, I'll take the couch," Kieran said. "Man, I wasn't expecting her to put us in the same room. That one kind of backfired on me." Amina hadn't even noticed the oversized, plush white couch in the center of the room. How much space did one person need for a bedroom? Still, even with all this space, it didn't change how awkward Amina felt about sharing a bedroom with a man she barely knew.

To Kieran's credit, he did everything he could to not look at Amina as she went through her nightly routine. He mumbled something about listening to a podcast and glued his attention to his phone. She snuck into the ensuite bathroom to change into her pajamas and wrap her hair for the night. When she returned, she noticed he was still staring at his phone.

"Night," she said lamely, not knowing what else to say.

"Night," he said back. She clicked off the lamp and did her best to fall asleep. Being in the same room as him felt wrong, yet she was anxious.

She ventured to close her eyes only when she was sure that he was completely out.

CHAPTER 6
Softening Affections

The morning was just as awkward as the night before. Amina was sure she would die from embarrassment. Both Kieran and Amina had the same idea of trying to avoid awkwardness by waking up earlier than the other. The only problem was that they both had the idea to set their alarm for seven in the morning. Still, they needed the cognition to realize the other person was in the room with them. The inevitable result was that they nearly crashed into each other trying to get ready.

"Sorry," Amina squeaked. The last thing she wanted was for him to see her in her baggy, worn-out pajamas. She had gotten up before him to get dressed in decent clothing for the day. Bristol had picked out a lovely polka-dot blouse with sheer sleeves and light capris for her.

"Don't worry about it." Kieran didn't seem as flabbergasted as her. But she couldn't shake her own nerves. She darted into the bathroom and quickly got dressed. Amina began worrying about how the day was going to go. She could make many mistakes that would give away what she and

Kieran were up to. She couldn't afford to slip up, not even once.

Ok. You can do this. Just remember what's on the line here. She looked at her reflection and nodded to herself. She could do this. Dropping the tension from her shoulders and taking a deep breath, she left the safety of the bathroom.

Kieran had already gotten dressed. Unlike the suit she usually saw him in at the cafe, he wore a light blue short-sleeved button-down and light linen pants.

"Hey, they just called up that breakfast is ready," Kieran said, gesturing to the bedroom door with his thumb. She had survived last night. Whatever the Hollands had in mind for the day had to be easier than the third degree they gave her last night.

She took Kieran's arm and did her best to give him her softest, most affectionate smile.

"Of course, darling," she said, tenderness oozing from her tone. Kieran flinched slightly and cleared his throat.

"Maybe don't lay it on quite that thick," he said with a touch of humor in his voice. They descended to the kitchen. The size of Kieran's family home still amazed her. She wondered how he could possibly walk around so easily and never feel like he was getting lost. They were welcomed into the kitchen by the warm sound of cheerful chatter.

When Kieran said breakfast was ready, Amina was maybe expecting scrambled eggs or pancakes. She wasn't expecting a whole freaking buffet laid out across a massive oak table. Mini pastries, assorted fruit, bacon, and the crème de la crème were the eggs benedict—homemade eggs benedict at that. Amina's stomach rumbled appreciatively. Kieran smirked at her, and she could have sworn she heard a slightly humorous chuckle in the back of his throat.

"Well, don't stand there like a stranger. Sit and eat," Esme said, gesturing at the spread. Amina didn't have to be told twice. She sat down, and her plate was loaded with good food. Amina hadn't had food this nice in a long time. When money got tight, her go-to meals were instant ramen, cereal, and her complimentary employee meal at A Cuppa Love.

"So, what have you rolled up your sleeves for today's activities?" Tori asked, tucking into a Danish with sheer delight. Amina followed suit and took a bite of the cherry Danish on her plate. It was tart and sweet.

"It's time for the fair maiden hunt," Scout said in a sing-song voice.

"I'm sorry, what's the fair maiden hunt?" Amina asked. Joyce giggled as she swirled her mimosa in her hand. Amina wondered briefly if she had one or two before they had breakfast.

"It's a game Scout's wedding planner came up with. All the girls in the bridal party hide, and the groom and groomsmen must find them." Amina suppressed the grimace that was forming on her face. What kind of archaic game is that?

"You should join too, Amina! Make that brother of mine do something fun for a change," Scout said.

"I am deeply wounded that you don't find me fun, dear sister," Kieran said, holding his hand to his chest and feigning offense.

"I don't know," Amina said. She didn't want to feel like a party pooper, but this game didn't exactly feel like her kind of thing. It sounded kind of... sexist.

"Oh, come on, it will be enjoyable, I promise," Scout said. Amina pressed her lip into a thin line. The last thing she wanted to do was play this game. It felt demeaning to make herself and the other women the "treasure" to be found. But if she didn't participate, the whole mood would be dampened. Or, at the very least, it would lead to Kieran having to do a lot of apologizing and explaining to his family. She glanced over at him and could practically hear him pleading with his eyes, *Please just go along with it.*

"Sure. Why not?" she said, forcing a smile. Scout beamed at her before she turned to her groom-to-be.

"I know the perfect hiding spot. You'll never find me," Scout said to Quincy with a competitive glimmer in her eyes.

"Don't be so sure," he said, giving her an equally teasing look. They quickly finished breakfast, and everyone gathered in the house's entryway. The wedding planner, whom Amina had just learned was named Joyce, lined the groom, grooms-men, and Kieran up and presented them with thick black blindfolds.

"Alright, the rules are straightforward. The gentleman will remain blindfolded, and the ladies will have five minutes to find a hiding spot," she explained. The rest of the women giggled, but all Amina could do was force a smile.

Before she could even blink, the blindfolds were used, and an enthusiastic "go!" was shouted. The bridal party scattered, and Amina blindly ran further into the house, quickly losing sight of the other women. *It feels like this game is a little stacked against me.* The house was so huge; Amina wasn't sure where to begin. Kieran and his sisters probably knew where every slight speck of dust in the house was.

She wracked her brain. Hiding behind the large curtains in the living room felt far too cliché. The garden outside was too well manicured for any decent hiding spots, and she was far from comfortable enough to hide in any of the bedrooms.

In her panicked wandering, she stumbled into the kitchen. *Well, I'm not crawling in the oven.* Then she spotted an odd-looking cupboard. She strained to listen, checking if she could hear anyone coming, but they echoed silently. She turned the latch, and the hinge groaned quietly in protest. As she opened the door, she realized the inside was much taller than it appeared. It took her a second before she realized what it was.

Amina covered her mouth to stifle the laugh that threatened to escape. Even despite the size of the house, the last thing she expected to find was a dumbwaiter. It was so stereotypical that it was almost hilarious. She examined it more closely. It was narrow but a bit bigger than she would have expected. She was confident she could fit if she scrunched her knees to her chest. It wouldn't be the most comfortable, but at least it would probably make for a good hiding spot. The narrowness served as a great advantage, after all. No one would expect her to attempt to squeeze in here.

She scooted onto the tray butt first. Her knees nearly touched her chin, but she managed to get the door shut, though she didn't latch it just to be on the safe side. The last thing she wanted was to get completely stuck.

She sat in the dark and sighed. This game is still dumb, but it's not so bad. She was glad to have a brief moment where she didn't have to pretend. Kieran's family so far were proving to be very lovely people. She hated lying to them, but what choice did she have?

From inside the dumbwaiter, she could hear Scout's bright laugh echoing through the mansion. If she had to hazard a guess, she'd say that Quincy found her first.

That didn't take too long. Guess he really knew her. For a moment, she wondered how long it would take Kieran to find her. On the one hand, this was his family's house. But would he look at the dumbwaiter and know she would hide there? As she pondered to herself, her back started to ache from the scrunched position she had to twist herself into to fit. If he didn't find her soon, she would get out and just let herself be seen.

As if sent by the universe itself, she heard the hinge of the dumbwaiter whine once again, and she was greeted by a familiar pair of light-colored linen pants.

"You do know that was probably a terrible idea, right?"

Kieran said as he helped her out. "You could have gotten stuck. Or if you weren't on the bottom floor, there's an excellent chance you could have fallen."

"Good thing I used my brain and realized I wasn't going to get stuck or fall," Amina retorted. She stretched out her back and sighed as everything unclenched. She was slim, but even for her, it was a very tight space to hide in. When she lowered her arms, she noticed Kieran was looking at her with an unreadable expression.

"What?"

After the game, the rest of the day was relatively uneventful. More and more family made their way to the manor, and many introductions were made. Amina couldn't keep track of all the distant cousins, aunts, and uncles. The following two days were going to be busy with the rehearsal dinner and the wedding itself.

A simple chicken dinner was served. The influx of extended family members made Amina feel even more self-conscious. More aunts, uncles, and cousins arriving meant more introductions and questions. She hadn't quite anticipated the size of Kieran's extended family.

"So, Amina, I don't think I asked—what is it that you do for a living?" Esme asked. Amina looked down at her napkin. She had been worried about these particular questions since she showed up. Kieran was successful, and the rest of his family did well for themselves. How was she supposed to answer that she was just a barista doing her best to survive at the best of times?

"Oh... um, I work at a cafe," she said, her voice much smaller than anticipated. One of Kieran's younger distant cousins snorted.

"Something funny, Drake?" Kieran asked with a surprising edge to his voice.

"Nothing, I'm just surprised. I always pictured you dating

a twig-thin supermodel, not a barista." The rest of the family looked deeply uncomfortable at Drake's comment. Esme had such a sharp, disapproving stare in Drake's direction that even Amina was flinching. She wondered if Esme was going to say something, but she noticed her attention turned to Kieran as if watching to see how he would respond.

"Well, I don't know about you, Drake, but I think Amina works twice as hard as you do scrolling on social media all day," Kieran said, feigning pleasantness in his voice. Drake opened his mouth to retort, but a death glare from Kieran's aunt and Esme silenced him quickly.

"Well, it isn't as fancy as what Kieran does, but I do have to admit, I love it," she said. Underneath the table, she gave Kieran's hand an appreciative squeeze.

"Good, as long as you work hard and enjoy what you do, then there's nothing wrong with that," Esme said authoritatively. The conversation quickly shifted to other topics, and Amina promptly felt more at ease.

After dinner, Amina needed some fresh air. Thankfully, near the dining room, there was a terrace. She inhaled the clear summer air appreciatively. She thought back to dinner and smiled. She hadn't expected that Kieran would stick up for her like that.

"You doing ok out here?" Kieran said from behind her. She turned and smiled at him.

"Yeah. Your family is very nice. I just needed a little bit of air," she said. He came up and joined her at the railing. She looked at him for a moment, trying to figure out how to convey that she appreciated what he did at the dinner.

"What?" Kieran asked, frowning in confusion. Amina hadn't realized she had been staring.

"Oh, nothing. Just thank you for that, by the way," she said, gesturing with her thumb back to the house.

"Oh, you're welcome. Look, I may be rich and successful

— probably more than any person needs to be—but I do know a thing or two about hard work. My whole family has been busting their asses to get to where we are today. A Holland works hard. Drake is just a young little shit who forgets that," Kieran said. Amina nodded thoughtfully. They were silent for a moment, but unlike before, it wasn't awkward. This time, it was more comforting.

"What would you do with your life if you could?" Kieran asked. Amina wasn't sure how to answer that. She had spent so many years focused on her sister that she had long forgotten her buried dreams.

"Well, I was in business school. I never really narrowed it down. It was going to be my own cafe or a restaurant or something," Amina said. "But things didn't work out quite the way I wanted them to, so... here I am."

"Well, for what it's worth, I think it matters more that you're a good person than what you do for a living. I've met many people from all walks of life, and many of them are out to get something. But you've never struck me as that kind of person. You're kind and—I don't know, I guess," Kieran said. Amina blushed furiously.

"You shouldn't sell yourself short either," she mumbled. She realized how close they were to standing together as she looked back at them. The air between them was crackling as if they were in for a thunderstorm. Except there wasn't a single cloud in the sky.

Amina couldn't have told anyone who moved first, but she was next aware of Kieran's lips pressing gently against hers. Heat and electricity coursed through every part of her body. She didn't know what she was doing. All she knew was that she didn't want to stop.

Kieran's Aunt Margaret stepped out onto the terrace, clearing her throat.

"Don't mind me. It's too stuffy inside for my old lungs."

Amina touched her lips where, just moments before, Kieran had been kissing. An electric tingle was still coursing through her body. As her shock slowly faded, a realization crept up on her.

Not only had she enjoyed that kiss, but she wanted Kieran to kiss her again. And again until she was left entirely dizzy. She had been distrusting and cautious, but now she couldn't deny it. But Kieran had made her feel welcome in his family. He stood up for her when his little shit of a cousin was trying to put her down. He paid enough attention to her that he knew seemingly frivolous pieces of information that showed he cared enough to learn about her.

She was attracted to Kieran Holland. She was actually starting to fall head over heels for him as well.

CHAPTER 7
Enticing Evening

Kieran woke up to the sound of the floorboards creaking. Peeking one eye open, he noticed Amina tiptoeing to the bathroom, clothes clutched in her arms. *I guess she's still shy about being in her pajamas around me.* He didn't know why. She looked beautiful in baggy purple shorts and a ratty gray T-shirt. Amina lightly closed the door with a soft click and turned the water in the shower on. With a groan, Kieran stood up, stretching out his back.

After tomorrow, he would return to his own house and sleep alone in his bed. The thought left Kieran's chest feeling hollow. They had only been sharing a room for a few days, but he somehow felt used to seeing her there. However, he had to admit that having her close to him tested his willpower terribly. He had been gentlemanly and restrained, but it had taken everything in him, especially after that kiss. Maybe it was their proximity to a bed, or perhaps he just found her even cuter in her pajamas. Either way, he had burned through his entire podcast library, trying to avoid making her uncomfortable.

Right as Kieran finished getting dressed, the shower faded into silence.

"Morning," Amina said as she stepped out of the bathroom. Her bouncy, natural curls were still dry.

"Morning," Kieran repeated with a smile. The two of them stood there for a moment, unsure what to say. Was he supposed to bring up the kiss or just ignore it?

"So... what's on the itinerary today?" Amina asked, rocking slightly on her heels.

"Well, today is the rehearsal dinner, so it's mostly the wedding party making sure everything is ready to go tomorrow. We have some time before then, though. How do you feel about checking out the town?" he asked. Rose Creek was admittedly small and easily missable on the map. Still, Kieran couldn't help but feel excited about showing Amina his home. Amina grinned at him.

"Sure, that sounds like fun," she said, smiling. There was something about her smile that reassured Kieran. He knew that she hadn't been overly comfortable around him at first. Not that he could really blame her for being all that guarded. True, he had learned a few things about her from coming into A Cuppa Love, but before the weekend, he had basically been a complete stranger to her. In her scenario, he wouldn't have trusted himself either.

"Alright, let's go. There's a great place to get some breakfast in the downtown area," he said. They drove into town, and he was genuinely surprised at how interested Amina was in explaining everything.

She inhaled her waffles with gusto, and they wandered around the downtown area for quite some time. Rose Creek may not have been that big, but they weren't above trying to attract as few tourists as they could. There were shops for the outdoorsy people who visited the nearby campgrounds and local stores that sold little tchotchkes and knick-knacks. But

Amina wanted to see all of it, so he took her arm and led her there. He thought back to when he was dating Nyra. She had only ever wanted to go places in the city with him. She never appreciated where he grew up like Amina did.

He noticed that she was staring into the window of the jewelry store. Unlike the other kitschy stuff that he entertained Amina with, this store was one of the few that catered more to people who came to Rose Creek to get a big house.

Curious, Kieran craned his neck to see what she was looking at. It was a small, thin gold chain studded with tiny rhinestones twinkling in the June sunshine. She wasn't looking at it greedily. In fact, it wasn't even the most audacious piece of jewelry the store had to offer. But there was a look of slight longing in her eyes.

"Do you like that bracelet?" he asked, motioning to the display window. Amina ducked her head, a slight blush blooming across her face, as if she felt wrong for wanting something so expensive and seemingly frivolous.

"It's beautiful and way out of my budget." Amina sighed. Before she could stop him, Kieran marched right into the store.

"Kieran! I can't let you buy that for me. It's way too much money!" she said as she trailed after him. He was far faster than her, however. When she caught up, he was already at the counter with his credit card.

"Oops. Too late," he said, suppressing the urge to laugh. He didn't suspect that Amina was the type to be materialistic. But he saw that look in her eyes when she looked at the bracelet.

"Kieran, come on. If I wanted it, I would get it," Amina said, folding her arms.

"Nice try, but I can tell that you want it. And you just said it's too much money for you," he said with a slightly cheeky smile. "If I have enough to burn a million on you for just coming with me this weekend, I think I can afford the bracelet."

Amina's eyes furrowed, and she folded her arms. Shit. Kieran hadn't meant to make her feel uncomfortable. Dropping his smile into a gentler one, he placed the jewelry box in her hand.

"Look, don't worry about it too much, ok? I'm buying you the bracelet because you want it, and I want you to have it. It's as simple as that."

"But what about the million?" Amina asked in a hushed tone.

"As I said, don't worry about it. Speaking of which, I also sent you the rest of the money. It's not like you'd back out anyways, and you've held up your end of the bargain," he said. He could tell Amina knew she wasn't going to win this argument. She dropped her arms and sighed, but she smiled softly.

"Fine, but only on one condition. You let me buy you an ice cream before we head back."

"Only if I get three scoops. Since it's your treat and all," Kieran said, grinning. Amina laughed, and Kieran felt like his insides were melting. He wanted to keep hearing her laugh and seeing her smile more openly. Her being more comfortable like this around him made him feel inexplicably happy.

"It's a deal," she said, shaking his hand.

Amina closed the clasp of her new bracelet around her wrist. She wasn't sure why, but when Kieran gave it to her, she could have sworn she felt her heart flutter for a brief moment. It wasn't really like her to get this flustered over a guy. Especially one she didn't really know, but she felt like she was getting to know him.

The rehearsal dinner went according to plan. The wedding

party practiced their entrances, exits, and all the other little intricacies that would go into the ceremony. Amina noticed the longing looks between Scout and Quincy. They looked at each other like they were tied together, as if they would simply float off into the void without the other. Amina couldn't help but wonder, if only for a moment, what Kieran felt when he looked at her.

The dinner itself was nothing to sneeze at, either. A hearty lasagna had been served, one of the best Amina had tasted in her entire life.

Joyce and Tori had the idea to start playing some music. It was relatively generic dinner music, a classier version of jazz than the jazz hop that often played at A Cuppa Love.

"Now this song takes me back to when your grandfather and I still went out dancing," Esme said, a wistful, longing look in her eyes.

"Now my knees are far too old for it. So, while you're young, you should dance while you can with the one you love," Esme sighed.

"Grandma, please. I'm not supposed to cry until tomorrow," Scout said, blowing her nose with her napkin. Amina had to agree. There was something profoundly romantic about the music. She couldn't keep herself from humming along to the tune. Other people were beginning to get caught up in the mood too, as slowly but surely, people were making their way to the more open areas to dance. Kieran looked at her with a smile before he stood up from the table.

"May I have this dance, Amina?" Kieran said, extending his hand to her. She took it and felt a tingle as their fingers interlocked. Amina knew how to dance a little, but she couldn't help but feel self-conscious with Kieran's entire family there. Kieran didn't seem fazed; however, he took her by the waist, and they moved through the steps as if they had been dancing together their whole lives. Amina's heart pounded, and she couldn't tear her eyes away from Kieran's face. His expression was soft, but there was also another look to it. A longing look—that she knew she was also reflecting back at him.

The music faded out, and they stood in the middle of the room for a while. Both of them waited silently for the other to make a sudden move. Amina knew she couldn't have been imagining it. They weren't just baristas and cafe regulars anymore. Something in the course of the weekend had changed. She couldn't pinpoint where or when, but she knew she didn't see Kieran quite the same way anymore. And she knew that she liked him.

The rehearsal dinner ended as quickly as it started. Scout said something akin to needing her beauty sleep, and Quincy pulled her close to him by the waist.

"Then you must have been comatose to be as beautiful as you are," he said softly, kissing Scout's cheek. Amina felt an odd, envious feeling settle in her chest. She wondered if Kieran was the type to say that kind of thing.

Climbing the stairs to their bedroom, Amina's heart pounded against her ribcage. Somehow, she felt more nervous than when they shared the room the first night. She couldn't place it, but she felt this sudden... anticipation. She clutched the hem of her skirt and hoped that Kieran hadn't noticed how odd she was probably acting.

Her fingers rested for a moment on the doorknob. Some-how, she knew that right now, things were different. There was some inexplicable force drawing her toward Kieran. She wanted nothing more than to lock the door behind them and find out how close they could get without things getting awkward. But the real question was, did he feel the same way?

She glanced back at him. Kieran had an odd expression in his eyes. A deep, aching physical yearning reflecting her own emotions back at her. She had never felt this way with anyone before. But they were only just getting to know each other. Were they really going to take that leap?

Screw it. I'm going to a wedding with a stranger for a million dollars. Her hesitation evaporating, she pressed a soft yet firm kiss on his lips. For a moment, Kieran stood rigid as if in shock. But soon, he pulled her closer by the waist. A tremor went through her body. Now there was definitely no second guessing. There was something between them—some kind of spark, electricity, or whatever Amina wanted to call it. She couldn't name it, but it was on the tip of her tongue.

"Um, hold on. Just remember, I have absolutely no idea what I'm doing," Amina said, ducking her head sheepishly. Kieran was aware that she was a virgin, but she couldn't help but feel like if she did something wrong, she would somehow spoil the moment.

His fingers rested gently under her chin as he tilted it so she looked directly at him.

"Just tell me if at any point you feel uncomfortable, and I'll stop. For now, though, just trust me," he said, bringing himself closer to her ear and breathing hotly. His teeth grazed the lobe, and she let out a small moan.

"Good girl," Kieran said. Another shiver razed Amina's spine. He kissed the edge of her collarbone, and she suppressed a moan. His hands moved up her neck and stopped on her cheek. She grabbed his wrist and led his hand up to her hair, where his fingers looped around her curls, gently tugging at them.

They collapsed onto the bed in a whirlwind of kissing, tender grazing with the teeth' soft caresses. Their legs intertwined, and when Kieran entered, Amina slightly dug her nails into the skin on his back. But soon, the discomfort faded, and Amina found herself melting into him. There was nothing but him and her and crickets on the summer night.

Amina lay in the bed, a wave of feelings she had never felt before hitting her all at once. She had finally had sex and made love. But as she rolled over, the only thing that greeted her was seeing an empty space on the bed where Kieran should have been.

He must just be getting ready for the ceremony, which is exactly what she should be doing.

The gown Bristol had chosen for her was far more formal than Amina had even dared to hold in her entire life. It was a deep violet A-line dress that ended just shy of her ankles and hugged her chest with a sweetheart neckline. For how dark the fabric was, the tulle of the skirt was surprisingly light and airy, a great comfort for the June sun.

She still couldn't find Kieran, which she found odd. Shouldn't they head to the church together? But she assumed he was probably just busy, seeing as he was the bride's brother. She managed to snag a ride to the church with one of his distant relatives, but still, she couldn't help but feel a flutter of anxiety.

The church was old but well maintained. Color sparkled across the room from the stained-glass windows. The aisle was brimming with various flowers—a sea of pink, purple, and white. Amina caught the scent of roses, lilacs, and baby breath wafting through the air—a heady and intoxicating scent.

Amina spotted Kieran, and he beamed at her. The anxiety she felt instantly settled.

"You look lovely," he said. Amina was about to reply but was soon thrown into another sea of intense introductions. To her surprise, Esme pointed out Kieran's ex-girlfriend with a snort of derision. She was a beautiful woman with sleek black hair, light brown skin, and curves that could have knocked a man flat.

"I'd steer clear of her if I were you, dear," Esme said, her voice taught with annoyance. Amina made a note of that. Kieran had gotten away from her at some point with all the pre-wedding socializing. Amina struggled to spot him, but when she did, her stomach dropped.

He was standing near the front with his ex-girlfriend Nyra hanging all over him.

She felt like she had been slapped. She blinked and was surprised to find that the corners of her eyes were wet. Blotting hastily with her hand, she did her best to compose herself, but all she wanted was to leave the wedding right then and there.

Amina had been so confident last night that there was something between her and Kieran. Now she was looking at his ex clinging to him like he had been there with her the whole time, and Amina was just a spare.

Whatever she had felt, she had been wrong.

CHAPTER 8
Wedding of Scorn

"Are you alright, Amina?" Esme said, tapping her on the shoulder. Amina inhaled sharply, but her throat was still tight and burning. Amina shook her head. She was there to do a job. So while she was doing the job, she would be the most romantic partner Kieran could have ever asked for. She wasn't going to ruin it by crying to his grandmother. She would hold up her end of the deal no matter what.

"Oh, I'm alright. Weddings just make me a bit sentimental." She sniffed. No one would question her getting emotional for a display of love and eternal commitment.

"I suppose I better find my seat," she said, plastering on a smile.

"Oh, don't be silly. You'll sit with the family," Esme said. Amina felt another tug at her heart. Esme was just being kind. She couldn't have known that what she said would make her feel a thousand times worse. If Amina were to try to explain that she was upset about Kieran and Nyra, maybe Esme would understand, but this was Scout and Quincy's day. Her feelings did not matter. Besides, what could she do at this point? Nothing except to continue to pretend.

The pastor announced that the ceremony would start soon, and they all filed in to take their seats. Kieran sat next to her with a large smile on his face. Amina mirrored it back, but all she wanted to do right at that second was scream at him.

The wedding party made their entrances, and soon Scout walked down the aisle. Amina couldn't help but feel a little envious. She had never given much thought to getting married. But the way Scout glided down the aisle in her gown, the look of rapture on Quincy's face—all of it was enough to make the biggest cynic a romantic. It also twisted the knife further when she knew Kieran would never look at her that way as long as Nyra was around.

The rest of the ceremony passed in a blur. The only thing she was actively aware of was when Kieran made a show of grabbing her hand and squeezing it. Her whole body went stiff.

"It was a charming ceremony," Amina smiled forcefully at Kieran. He turned to her, but a ping from his phone turned his attention away from her.

"Sorry. It's some kind of work emergency at one of the factories. I gotta take this," he explained. Without another word, he promptly got up and left Amina alone in the pew.

What the heck was that? She felt the threat of tears begin again and promptly left to find the church bathroom.

Once she got there, she gripped the edge of the sink tightly. She carefully blotted some cold water on her face with the paper towel. It would be a shame to ruin the makeup she had been carefully instructed to replicate. Analyzing her face carefully in the mirror, she wondered if something was wrong with her. Had she bored or offended Kieran somehow? But before she could conclude, Nyra came into the bathroom with a smug smile. Amina suppressed the urge to groan. Nyra is the last person I want to see right now.

"You must be Amina! I'm Nyra," Nyra said in a sickeningly sweet sing-song voice. She held her hand as if asking Amina to shake or kiss it. Amina kept her hands on the sink, and Nyra dropped her hand and only smiled wider. Everything about her body language seemed to ooze insincerity.

"Nice to meet you," she said. She pulled herself from the sink and tried to leave the bathroom, but Nyra stood in the doorway.

"You know, Kieran and I used to date," Nyra said, a sudden edge to her voice. Play it cool, Amina. Play it cool.

"That is very interesting," Amina said calmly.

"Kieran isn't the settling-down sort. Once he gets a good one in the sack, he's done," Nyra said, her white teeth flashing unnaturally bright in the bathroom's fluorescent light. Amina felt bile trying to climb its way up her throat, and she forced herself to swallow. Nyra was definitely trying to get a rise out of her, but it wasn't going to work.

"I wouldn't get too excited about the bracelet," Nyra said, extending her hand again. On her wrist was a very similar, delicate chain bracelet. Amina felt the acid clawing its way up her throat.

"I'll keep that in mind," Amina said flatly. Despite the prickling at the corners of her eyes, she would not cry in front of Nyra. Something about how she was grinning over Amina, like a cat playing with a wounded bird, did not sit well with her.

She's trying to get a rise out of you. Don't react. That's precisely what she wants. But no matter how much Amina repeated, she couldn't help but feel defeated.

She excused herself from the bathroom. Everything after that passed in a blur. Kieran never said a word to her in the car on the way to the reception hall. He had been far too busy yelling into his cell phone. He only seemed to pause for breath when the dinner was served. Amina kept smiling and only contributed to the conversation when necessary.

When the dancing started, Kieran disappeared quickly to yell into his phone even more. Amina sighed. Everyone else was socializing and having fun; here she was a complete wall-flower because her "date" was ignoring her.

She wondered if he was being aloof because he got exactly what he wanted from her. Despite her "no sex" clause, she had been the one to cave. Maybe he had been expecting her to, or that was his plan from the beginning. Now that he got what he wanted, he was being aloof. Throwing her away, so to speak, now that he was done with her.

Needless to say, she felt humiliated. She had enough self-respect that she desperately wanted to leave. She didn't deserve this. But whenever she thought about getting up and leaving, she wondered how Kieran or the rest of the Hollands would react. But then she saw Kieran with Nyra on the dance floor. Her heart stopped for a brief second before sinking onto the laminated dance floor. That was the final straw.

Aggressively, she put her glass back down on the table. Amina didn't even try to look at Kieran anymore.

Once she got outside, the tears she had been forcing back finally broke free. She was an idiot. She should never have trusted Kieran, she should never have come here with him, and she definitely should have never caught feelings. She laughed dryly, wondering if it would have hurt less to have sex with a total stranger like she had initially planned to do.

Her phone rang shrilly from her small clutch purse. *Perfect, this is exactly what I need right now.* Fumbling through her clutch, she finally pulled it out. She half expected it to be Kieran, but it wasn't. Why would he suddenly care anyways? But when she took a second look, she felt a cold shiver dance down her spine. It was the hospital her sister was staying at. Immediately, she clicked the answer button.

"Hello. Is this Amina Bethune?" the voice on the other end of the phone sounded slightly breathless and hurried already—not a good sign.

"Speaking," Amina said, feeling her guts twist not with heartbreak and sadness but with deep anxiety.

"I'm calling from Woodland Medical Hospital. I'm afraid your sister has taken a little bit of a turn. It's nothing serious at the moment, but we were told to inform you," the voice continued.

"Of course. I'll be right there," she said, hurriedly hanging up to book a cab. Getting back to Portland from here would be costly, but she didn't care.

She quickly checked her phone's banking app. She was surprised that Kieran kept his word and sent her the money for some reason. She hadn't felt the need to check when he told her, but seeing the large number on her screen somehow made her feel worse.

So, this was it. Their deal was good and done for. Serena needed her, and nothing else tied her to Kieran or the rest of the Hollands. Her hand trembling, she called a cab.

It took ages for the cab to arrive. Amina thought for sure someone would have come and found her. But she was left sitting at the front entrance, her heels in her hands, trembling with anger and sadness.

The cab pulled up with a cheerful honk that juxtaposed Amina's melancholic mood. She slid into the backseat, gave the driver the address, and sat silently.

Despite herself, she didn't want to leave Kieran completely hanging without a word. As they drove off, she hurriedly texted him that she had a family emergency. She wondered if he would even notice the message. The only things that seemed to be holding his attention right now were work and

Nyra. Minutes ticked by, and there wasn't even as much as a read message. That settled it, then. He didn't give two shits about her.

She would forget everything about Kieran. They had both held up their end of the bargain. She owed him nothing, and he owed her nothing. Amina knew she had made the right decision by leaving.

And yet, more tears were trickling down her cheeks as she leaned against the cab window.

CHAPTER 9
Time Marches On

Four Months Later

Amina fumbled for her keys, a hint of nausea in her stomach. She couldn't afford to run late. She would lose her job if she kept running late because she couldn't stop throwing up in the morning.

"You ok?" Serena called out sleepily from the bedroom doorway. Amina didn't ever want to get used to hearing her sister's voice in the apartment. After all, it was a constant reminder that she was getting better every day. Kieran's money had not only helped with Serena's heart and double lung transplant but also with the extended hospital stay she had to endure afterward. It had been a long and arduous recovery. Needless to say, they had quickly blown through the money Kieran had given Amina. An extended stay plus all the medications Serena needed post-transplant—well, without insurance, it added up very quickly. Amina had been prepared for that.

What Amina hadn't been prepared for, however, were two total gut punches from the cruel design of fate. First, A Cuppa Love had closed. Maren's health continued to decline until the staff was notified that she had inevitably passed away. Maren never left the cafe to anyone in her will, so naturally, the bank seized it. That, Amina knew she could survive. There were an endless number of cafes she could apply to in Portland.

She didn't know how to deal with the second surprise. Amina was pregnant. When she found out, she sat in the apartment living room with Serena and cried. She felt like an idiot and told Serena everything about Kieran and the wedding. Serena was a bit angry. Amina had put herself through that for her sake, but she sat with her and comforted her.

But after she picked herself up off the floor, Amina knew what she wanted to do. It wasn't ideal, but she decided to keep the baby. It wasn't their fault for what had happened. But she wouldn't be able to do it without making any money. Serena still couldn't work despite being home. She was on her own once again. At least she was used to it by this point. With the little money she had left from Kieran, she got herself a cart and made a deal to sell coffee and pastries in a corporate office building.

Kieran sighed. He came up on another dead end when searching for Amina. He had been looking for four months and had come up completely empty. All he knew was that she had to leave for an emergency. But when he tried to contact her later, he found out she had utterly blocked his number. Even visiting A Cuppa Love had been a cold trail. He couldn't believe it when he found the foreclosure sign on the door.

Now he was reduced to looking through social media while at work. He was surprised that she didn't seem to have any accounts whatsoever. Either that, or she was very good at hiding all her profiles. He groaned and wanted to put his head on his desk. He was beginning to lose hope. He'd never see Amina or taste her amazing Cortados again.

"Here's your Cortado, sir," Hannah, Kieran's assistant, said, placing the cup on his desk. He nodded appreciatively and took a long sip.

There was something oddly familiar about the taste of the coffee. If Kieran hadn't known better, he could have sworn it tasted exactly like the Cortado Amina used to make at A Cuppa Love. But it couldn't be.

Could it?

Kieran cursed under his breath. Of course, that meeting had to take almost two hours longer than expected. It could have all been an email, but no, *they love to see me suffer.* Now he would be stuck at the office until late this evening. *Good thing I called Hannah to get me another Cortado.*

As he was about to enter the building, something caught his eye. He felt like a splash of cold water had been thrown at him. Walking away from him was Amina. He had been looking for her for so long, and she was right before him.

He had always wondered what actually happened that night. She didn't talk about her family that weekend, and a guilty part of him wondered if she had somehow faked the emergency just to run off with his money. *It shows I should have paid the second half after the reception.*

Still, she left him with much explaining to do with his family. And yet he couldn't help but feel glad to see her. He opened his mouth to call out her name, but it was then that he noticed she wasn't alone. Walking next to her was a guy. He only saw the back of him, which was maddening.

He couldn't help but feel a stab of regret. He was happy to see her, but it hurt him to think she was with somebody. At least he knew then that she hadn't been mysteriously kidnapped at the reception. But that still didn't squash his envy.

As he entered the office, Hannah handed him his coffee. He took a sip, and a realization dawned on him. He saw Amina near the building, and twice now, he's had coffee that tasted just like hers. It couldn't just be a coincidence.

"Hannah, you said you got this from the cafeteria, right?" Kieran asked.

"Yeah, a girl comes in daily with a cart now," she said. Kieran grinned. He had finally found her.

The next day, he knew he had to see it with his own eyes. He came to work early and scoured the cafeteria. And there she was. He had been so busy that it was no wonder he hadn't seen the cart in the cafeteria, but he still found himself stunned. She looked just as beautiful as the first day he saw her at A Cuppa Love. Any resentment from that weekend melted like snow on the first day of spring.

Feeling bold, he walked up to the cart.

"I'll take a Cortado," he says. A flash of recognition darted across Amina's face as she lifted her head to meet Kieran's eyes. Startled and distracted, the hot coffee spilled, some of it landing on her hand.

Amina yelped and grabbed an ice cube from the tray to soothe the tiny burn mark.

"What are you doing here?" she asked incredulously. Kieran could have asked her the same question. In fact, he could have asked her a million questions. Why did you leave the wedding and completely ghost me? Is the problem you had with the money solved now? What happened to Cuppa Love?

But for some reason, none of those questions could escape his lips. Maybe he wasn't ready to ask them, or he didn't want to overwhelm her more than he already had.

"I work here in the building," he said. He wondered for a

moment if he should ask her about the wedding. But this was hardly the circumstance to ask such a personal question. For one thing, a small line began forming behind him.

No, he would have to act friendly, at least for now. She'd be more likely to answer him honestly if he could prove she didn't have to be so guarded around him.

"Interesting," she said, her voice trembling ever so slightly. Not only that, but her eyes were darting around erratically as if she was looking for an escape. He couldn't figure out why she seemed to be deathly afraid of him right now. Sure, he wasn't thrilled that she skipped out of the reception, but he wouldn't yell at her about it. Certainly not while she was working, at any rate. More than anything, he just wanted a chance to understand what had happened.

What on earth is going on with her? She runs out of the wedding, doesn't contact me for months, and now acts like she's afraid to see me. Not only that, but her usual pleasant nature felt much more stilted and forced, as if she was just talking to a customer who complained that the croissants were too dry and she just took them out of the oven.

Kieran knew something was up with Amina. And he was going to find out what. One way or another.

CHAPTER 10
Keeping Secrets

Amina couldn't believe her eyes. The last person she expected to see in this building was Kieran. She didn't want to see him. *Can he tell I'm pregnant? What do I say to him if I am?* A thousand more questions rattled inside her skull. But with all the other customers in line behind Kieran, this was hardly the time or the place to think about it. Besides, if he didn't suspect anything, her acting weird would just tip him off that something was off.

"Right. One Cortado coming right up," she said. He raised his eyebrow at her, but she turned her attention to the coffee machine. If he was another customer, she'd be able to focus on making the drink and block his presence out. But this time, she couldn't help but sneak a glance at him to watch his expression. She was looking for any subtle shift in his face that told her he was mad about the wedding or that he knew she was pregnant. She prayed her apron was enough to hide the baby bump. Her hands shook as she prepared his Cortado, and she had to breathe to avoid burning herself all over again.

"How have you been?" he asked as she poured the hot water over the espresso.

"Fine," she choked. She wondered if he would ask her why she ran out on him. Hell, she expected it. But he just... stood there, watching her. Her hands trembled as she got the Cortado ready, and she prayed that he didn't notice how afraid she was of him being there.

It wasn't necessarily that she was afraid of him, per se. She didn't expect him to hurt her, but how would he react if he found out about the baby? She didn't expect his reaction to be positive if he truly wasn't the family type. Even if it was, it's not like she wanted him around anyway. As far as she was concerned, she would have been delighted to care for it entirely alone and never see Kieran Holland for as long as she lived.

But for whatever reason, fate had made them cross paths once again. Clearing her throat, she put the lid on the cup and handed it to him. He took it with a tight but grateful smile.

"Hey, are you alright?" he asked in a hushed tone. He leaned closer to her, and she wanted to punch him for touching her counter.

"You kind of left the wedding in a hurry," Kieran continued. She wanted to laugh. Why was he acting like he cared about her running off? If he hadn't been so busy grinding against Nyra, maybe she would have been a bit more forgiving of him. But even right now, as he acted like nothing happened —that it was all on her for ditching him—it made her even more angry.

Granted, she couldn't afford to be as rude to him as she would have liked. Whether she liked it or not, he was still, at the moment, a paying customer. It took her far too long to get this cart and start earning back the money she lost. If she wanted to keep surviving, she would have to play nice. And as

Kieran already knew, she was an expert at playing nice and sweet.

"Yeah, sorry. It really was a family emergency," she said as she put the cardboard sleeve around the cup. She hoped he didn't think she was lying about that. That part had at least been accurate. But how else was she supposed to explain that she caught feelings for him and he crushed them in a matter of hours? Not that he even deserved to know.

He took the cup from her and hung it there awkwardly. She didn't like the way he stared at her as if he was somehow trying to analyze her feelings. *Good thing he can't because I want nothing more than to splash the Cortado all over him.*

"It was nice to see you again Amina," he said. Her skin erupted with goosebumps. She shivered as their hands made contact when she handed him the cafe Cortado.

"You too," she said tersely. She glanced behind him at the other customers in line, wondering if they noticed how awkward this interaction was. However, to her relief, nobody seemed to be paying that much attention. She turned her attention back to Kieran, who waved at her as he turned to leave.

"Well, take care," he said. With a smile and an arrogant saunter, he walked towards the elevator. Amina would have screamed if there wasn't a customer directly behind Kieran asking for a red eye.

"Coming right up," she said, oozing her customer service voice into every syllable. She tried to put Kieran out of her mind. But no matter how much she focused on work, she couldn't help but glance towards the elevator outside the cafeteria. Anytime it made its distant ping, her eyes darted in that direction as if she was expecting Kieran to come sprinting at her, demanding answers.

At least he didn't seem to be aware of her pregnancy. For that, she could let out a sigh of relief. It didn't do much to ease

Amina's anxiety, though. No matter how much she told herself it was better that he didn't know, she couldn't help but imagine what would happen if he did find out.

If she were right about Kieran, he would probably dip out the second he found out. Nyra had said that the family and commitment lifestyle was his thing. There was no sense in getting her hopes up where there were none. Or even worse, with how rich he was, maybe he would try to sue her for some case of entrapment. After all, she had been dumb and neglected to get birth control under the assumption that she wasn't planning on having sex anytime soon. But when she had all of Serena's medical bills to pay, her thoughts about her health were far from her mind.

Amina left early that day. She didn't want to risk running into Kieran again when he got off work. Not that she could say what time that would be. Still, it wasn't a risk that she was willing to take. She walked back to the apartment, still unable to shake the sight of Kieran from her mind.

Briefly, she wondered if she should quit and move her cart somewhere else. She quickly shook that thought off. It would take far too long to find somewhere to move the cart. He would win if she ran with her tail between her legs. At the same time, however, the longer she stayed, the more likely he would be to find out about the baby. She couldn't hide the bump behind an apron forever.

Amina got up to her apartment and paused in front of the door. She stood there for a moment, trying to banish all further thoughts of Kieran Holland from her mind. She smiled, opened the door, and called out a cheerful greeting to Serena. Serena glanced up from the book she was reading, and immediately, her smile dropped.

"Are you ok? You seem very tense," Serena said.

"I'm fine," Amina said, trying to wave Serena off, but Serena only frowned. She leaned over her knees and folded her hands expectantly, one still clutching onto the novel she was reading. It looked like there was no way Amina could lie her way out of this one.

"I ran into my baby daddy," Amina blurted out. Serena dropped her book. The two sisters stared at each other briefly before Serena slowly picked up her novel from the floor.

"That rich guy? How?" Serena asked. Amina explained everything to Serena, the words pouring out quickly as the panic she had been suppressing surged to the surface.

"You told him the baby was his, didn't you?" Serena prodded when Amina had finished.

"No. He didn't even see my stomach. He doesn't know I'm pregnant," Amina said quietly. Serena's eyes shot upward. She leaned closer to Amina and clasped her hands tightly together.

"I really think you need to tell him. I disagree with your plan of not telling him about the baby in the first place," Serena said. Amina had been very upfront with Serena, saying that if she could help, she planned on keeping Kieran out of the picture, even if it meant not telling him. Serena hadn't been thrilled with what Amina did to pay for her surgery, but she had been less thrilled when Amina said she didn't want Kieran to know about the pregnancy.

"Please, can we not start this discussion again?" Amina asked. Her feet were sore, and she was tired from running into Kieran's fiasco. All she wanted was to sit down and have a cup of tea.

"I'm just saying I think he would want to know," Serena pointed out. Sure, it was easy for Serena to say that. But she would have thought differently if she had been there when Nyra had that conversation with her at the reception.

"I've been told Kieran isn't the type to settle down and have a family type. Besides, after everything, if I tell him I'm pregnant, he will think I tried to trap him or something. Or I used him for the money, and now I'm going to use the baby to blackmail him or sue. Trust me; it's just better that he never finds out about the baby," Amina said.

Serena shook her head but didn't press the issue. Amina knew Serena was just trying to look out for her in her own way. But whenever she tried to picture Kieran finding out, all the scenarios were negative. So, her resounding answer was still "no." She had already resolved that she would do this on her own. It didn't matter that she didn't have the dad in the picture. She could do it by herself. She had to do it by herself to protect herself and the baby.

She didn't have any other choice.

CHAPTER 11
The Unexpected Discovery

Kieran couldn't get Amina out of his head. Ever since he saw her yesterday, he knew that something was up. She acted very differently from her usual easy-going, kind, and genuine self. What confused him even more was that he knew she was hiding something from him. While he excused her being guarded at first during the wedding weekend, he thought she was opening up to him. She abruptly leaves without saying anything, and when he locates her once more, she's acting nervous and evasive. Does it have something to do with what she needed the money for? Did she pretend to go along with his plan, and once she got her money, she decided to ditch him? He couldn't figure it out, and it was driving him mad.

He wanted to know what was happening with her and why she acted so nervous around him lately. More than anything, though, she just wanted to see her again. He hated that things were so weird between the two of them now. He missed her looking at him with that warm, friendly smile when she made him his coffee or when they were having fun with wedding games and touring his hometown. Looking back, he may have contributed to the problem by not checking in with her more at the wedding. But with work constantly buzzing his phone and Nyra insisting on talking to him, he couldn't catch a breath before realizing she had left the venue.

If he could, he hoped to make it right and at least get back on friendly terms again.

He would have to do this delicately; however, if he approached her too aggressively, he wouldn't get an answer out of her. He needed to get her used to seeing him again. Remind her that they had a good time at the wedding. And admittedly, he wanted another one of her cafe Cortados.

He made his way down to the cafeteria, surprisingly nervous. He wanted to see her again but wasn't sure how to bring any of this uncomfortable stuff up. There was a good chance they would get even more awkward if they tried to talk things out. Either way, they wouldn't get anywhere if they didn't talk about it. And if they were going to work in the same building, they would have to address it eventually. They were both adults, after all. Kieran was sure they could reach an amicable resolution if they just talked it through. But first, he had to get her used to seeing him again. Once he got her to relax around him again, he was confident she'd be more open to talking.

There was a lot more whispering in the cafeteria than he had anticipated. From what he could overhear, many people were surprised that he came down to get his coffee. He rolled his eyes. Could a man not get coffee without it turning into a whole ordeal? He had sent Hannah a couple of times for him because he was swamped with emails and a new ad campaign after all. Well, Kieran would have come down sooner if he had known Amina was working there.

He saw Amina at the cart from a side view. She was artfully arranging the pastries in the display case. Her apron was slung across the counter as she fumbled with the pastry boxes in her arms. The box nearly slipped, and she struggled to catch it and set it on the counter.

"Here, let me help you with that," he said after rushing to assist her. He reached down to grab the pastry boxes before she could protest.

That was when Kieran noticed Amina's stomach. She wasn't wearing her apron quite yet, and he couldn't help but notice that her stomach was bigger than when he last saw her.

Kieran stared at her for a long moment. At first, he wondered if she had simply gained weight. But the other part of his brain was screaming at him that this was not merely weight gain. This was another thing altogether, and it was something that made him feel like his heart had briefly stopped.

"Are you... pregnant?" he choked. Amina opened and closed her mouth several times, and her face had gone pallid.

"Yes," she said, her voice timid and quiet. She must have been far too shocked to deny it. Mentally, he calculated until he reached the foregone conclusion. Given how far along she looked, if he did his math correctly, there was a very strong probability that the baby was likely his.

"Is it mine?" he whispered. Amina opened and closed her mouth, but no sound came out. No denial of it came out either. Before Amina could answer, four gentlemen in suits walked up to the cart.

"Four cinnamon buns, please," one of the guys said, placing down the money. Amina gave Kieran an odd look before turning back to her other customers. It was amazing to Kieran how quickly she could drop her shit and turn on customer service mode. If he didn't know any better, he might as well have been talking to her about the weather.

"I'll talk to you later then," he said flatly. He walked away from the cart in a slight daze. He couldn't even recall the trip back up to his office. He sat back at his desk and stared blankly at his computer screen.

When Amina had a spare moment between rushes, she felt the panic finally set in. Kieran knew she was pregnant. And he most definitely suspected that the baby was his.

She put her "be back in five minutes" sign and retreated to the nearest bathroom. Thankfully, no one else seemed to need the facility at the moment. Doing her best not to hyperventilate, she took her phone out and dialed the only person who could help her right now.

"Hello?" Serena's voice had a slight panic to it. Amina didn't usually call her sister at work. If it were slow, she would text but only really leave phone calls for essential matters or dire emergencies. And this was a dire emergency.

"I ran into Kieran again. He knows I'm pregnant. He asked me if it was his, but I couldn't answer, and I got interrupted by a customer, and now I don't know what to do," Amina blurted.

"Ok. It's ok. Amina, just take a deep breath, ok?" Serena said. Amina did as she was instructed. It was a little odd having Serena walk her through something like this. Amina had spent so much time taking care of Serena. It felt weird having Serena take care of her right now.

"I know I keep saying this, but you must tell him. He deserves to know about his kid. He deserves to know his kid, and the baby deserves to know his father." Amina hated to admit it, but Serena was right. She hadn't stopped considering what keeping Kieran out of the loop might do to the child. In truth, she had only really been worried about protecting herself from an awkward conversation.

"But what if he doesn't want to be part of this? I don't

know him that well. We just... made a mistake at his sister's wedding. He wouldn't want to settle down and play 'Dad' out of the blue."

"Look, if he doesn't want to be part of the picture, that's his choice. But he has to be the one to make that decision, not you," Serena said. Amina wished she could believe it, but she wasn't so certain.

⁋⊱————⊰⁋

It took Kieran a while to snap out of his daze. But when he did, he knew the first thing he needed to do. There was no telling how having a kid would affect his business or public image. So he needed to get some kind of protection in place.

Searching through his phone, he found the number for his best friend, Dru. Thank God he went to law school. The phone rang for several minutes before he finally heard the disembodied voice of his friend.

"Hey, Kieran, what's up?" Drew asked, his voice cheerful.

"Hey, Dru. Look, man, I'm in a bit of a situation," he said. He very quickly explained the whole situation to him.

"Jesus Christ," Dru said. At least Kieran wasn't the only one shocked by the situation anymore.

"What are my options here?" Kieran asked. He couldn't honestly say what he wanted, but he needed to know there was an out.

"Ok, well, she's too far along to discuss if she's open to alternative options," Dru said. Kieran felt a slight tug in his chest. He knew where Dru was coming from.

"But if you need to confirm whether or not it's actually yours, I won't make any move until you find that out. After that, we can start, depending on what you want to do here. If you don't want to pay child support, we can get her to waive your parental rights." Kieran sighed and let the tension finally drop from his shoulders. He thanked Dru and packed up for the day.

As he was about to drive off, he saw Amina leaving the building. The shock had now thoroughly worn off, and he felt emboldened. He screeched the car to a halt right in front of Amina and rolled the window down.

"Get in," Kieran ordered.

"What? Why?" Amina asked.

"Just—please get in," he repeated a little more sharply than he had intended. Amina stood there with her arms folded for a moment. When she saw that Kieran wouldn't budge, she sighed and slid into the passenger seat.

"So, instead of being a jackass, you want to tell me what the hell is going on?" Amina asked as she clicked the seatbelt into place. While he had been full of bravado when he pulled up, he couldn't help but feel an anxious knot in his chest. If he asked her and got an answer, it would make the whole thing real.

"Is the kid mine?" he asked.

"Is that what this is about? Yes, the baby is yours," Amina said irritably. Kieran swallowed the lump that suddenly formed in his throat.

"I'm sorry, but I will still need to verify that information," Kieran said. Amina scoffed indignantly next to him.

"And what exactly do you mean by that?' Amina asked. Kieran rolled his eyes.

"I'm taking you for a damn paternity test." Amina made an incredulous noise in the back of her throat.

"I was a virgin when I slept with you!" Amina shrieked. Kieran dug his nails into the wheel of the car. Telling her he suspected she slept around after sex would likely lead to a fiery car crash. Kieran didn't particularly fancy dying that day, as miserable as he was.

"Yes, but it's been four months," he pointed out. "At least

try to understand this from my point of view," he said. Amina glared at him and pressed her lip into a thin line.

"Fine," Amina said frostily. She folded her arms over her chest, and they quietly drove to the hospital.

It took them a while to be seen. Amina kept staring daggers at him while they sat in the waiting room. It didn't help that their doctor seemed utterly oblivious to the tension crackling in the air. He kept trying to be far more amicable than either Kieran or Amina had the energy for.

"Okey, dokey. Well, we'll just get the test started, then. Would you like the gentleman in the room with you?" the doctor asked, looking at Amina.

"No, thank you," she mumbled. Kieran didn't have it in him to argue. He returned to the waiting room and paced the floor so much that the nurse at the counter had to ask him to take a seat as he was making other patients antsy. Soon, the doctor came out with Amina.

"Ok, we'll just send the results back to the lab. You two have a great day!" he said cheerily. Amina half-heartedly waved a hand at him and sighed.

"I wanna go home," she said to Kieran wearily. She looked exhausted beyond measure, and Kieran couldn't help but feel a little guilty for dragging her there.

"I'll take you home. If the kid is mine, I want you and them to be safe," he said. He still wasn't sure if he even wanted this kid until he decided he might as well ensure it was safe.

"Alright," Amina agreed. Wearily, she followed him to the car. Kieran kept stealing glances back at her on the drive to her apartment. Her head was pressed against the window, and her eyes were shut tight.

"Thank you for humoring me," Kieran said, attempting to be appreciative. Now that his adrenaline had worn out more, he wondered if he had been too aggressive with his insistence on the paternity test.

"Mhmm. It's your next right," Amina said, pointing to her neighborhood. When Kieran turned into the area, his nose involuntarily scrunched in disgust. This place was filthy. There was trash everywhere on the street, a gaggle of women who were most definitely prostitutes, and a whole host of the shadiest-looking people Kieran had ever seen.

"I gave you a million dollars, and this is where your apartment is? What kind of dump are you living in?" he balked. "If I went looking, I could probably find a hundred discarded needles without even trying."

Amina turned to him with a look that was full of venom.

"Oh, I'm sorry, I don't live in a big ass mansion and come from a long line of generational wealth," she spat.

"Oh, come on, Amina. You can't possibly stay here. It can't be good for you or the baby," he said, gesturing broadly outside. Amina unclicked her seatbelt and got out of the car. Instead of walking away, she leaned down so Kieran could see her glaring at him.

"If you must know, I spent that money caring for my sick sister's medical bills. So, I'm sorry that I don't live somewhere that fits your standards, but this is the reality for countless other people like me. So what else am I supposed to do? Live with you?" she said. Kieran's jaw hung open, but he didn't get a chance to reply before Amina slammed the car door and stormed off.

Well, that was an effective way to make him feel like an asshole. In all seriousness, though, he did feel a bit bad that he had trashed her neighborhood so harshly after she said all that. He had no idea she had a sister or was even that sick. He couldn't imagine the load that would leave on a person. No wonder Amina needed a lot of money.

But at the same time, it wasn't exactly like he was overly thrilled about Amina living there when she may or may not be carrying his child. What kind of environment was that? And if the million was spent on medical bills, how on earth would she afford to care for a kid?

Kieran leaned his head against the steering wheel and sighed. Things were so complicated out of nowhere. He sat in the car for a long time before returning home in complete silence.

That night, Kieran slept fitfully. All he could think about was the results of the paternity test. What would he do if Amina was having his kid? The last thing he had planned for was fatherhood. The very idea of it made the contents of his stomach swirl uncomfortably. Saying he wanted to throw up may have sounded dramatic, but he genuinely couldn't think of another way to describe it.

Unknowingly, memories of his father came flooding back to him. He rose and blasted himself with cold water in the shower to banish the unwanted memories. The last thing he needed in this situation was to think about his parents. They were his previous examples of model parenthood, after all. He never even knew if he wanted kids. If the kid was his, what was he going to do? How was he going to help Amina raise it? Would he help Amina raise it? And how soon would he mess up the kid for good if he did?

As he crawled back into bed, he hoped that Amina was lying. However, he had no reason to believe she would lie; deep down, he knew the truth. Amina was pregnant with his baby, and soon the tests would prove him right.

CHAPTER 12
Resolutions

Kieran still couldn't believe this. Amina was pregnant. A deep sense of anxiety and dread filled his stomach. He barely got any sleep the night before. He needed to clear his head to figure out what he was supposed to do.

He would be too restless at home, so he drove to his grandmother's house instead. He was reluctant to tell her about the baby. All he had managed to say to the family was that he and Amina had broken up shortly after the wedding, and he left it at that. But he knew that visiting her would at least help put all thoughts of Amina and the babies far behind him.

"Hi, Grandma," he said, giving her a hug as he walked in. She smiled and made him tea. He sat with her for a moment, trying to talk about anything and everything, but he noticed her looking at him oddly.

"Is everything alright, Kieran?" she said, putting her teacup down.

"Of course, Grandma," he said. But his grandmother narrowed her eyes at him.

"Nice try, but I know you better than that," she said.

Kieran shrugged. He wanted to talk about it, but he had no idea how she would react. When she saw she wouldn't get an answer from him, his grandma sighed.

"I know you don't want to talk about it, but that's ok. I raised you and your sisters. I know who you are deep down. You're a good man, unlike your father," she said.

"Grandma, what do you mean by that?" he asked. He was utterly taken aback by her dismissiveness of her late son. She shook her head sadly.

"Call it intuition. I just know it's what you need to hear right now. You think I don't notice a lot, but I do. I know you get awkward around women you date after a while, and I think I know where it's coming from. Your father, God rest his soul, was not a good father. He fell to his vices when times were hard, and it nearly ruined us all," she said.

"I don't want to talk about that right now," Kieran said firmly. He didn't like talking about his parents. He had very few memories of them, but the few he had were not happy ones. He could still hear their shouting echoing across the mansion as Scout tried to distract him, Joyce, and Tori so they would ignore it. Or how his grandmother would scream at the two of them to get things together for the sake of their children.

"I think you need to talk about it. If not with me, with somebody. I don't want you to get in your way when it comes to finding love." He wished she would stop. Maybe getting involved with Amina was a mistake in the first place. He knew she adored Amina when he brought her home for the wedding.

But he didn't want to have this conversation right now. He didn't like how thinking of his parents made bile rise in his throat or his heartbeat thump erratically. It was in the past. They were both gone, so he shouldn't waste a single hair worrying about them and how they affected him in his early childhood.

Kieran's grandmother seemed to understand she wouldn't get much more out of him. Shaking her head, she sighed and stood up, grabbing a small watering can that Kieran hadn't noticed earlier.

"Well, you've done right by your sisters and me all these years. I'm sure you'll do right by your future family," his grandma said as she walked into the conservatory to tend to her rose bushes.

It always scared Kieran how accurate his grandmother's intuition was. He didn't know how she knew, but he suspected that she was more aware that he got Amina pregnant than he had anticipated. Why else would she suddenly bring up my parents and all that talk about doing right by his family?

He drove to work and couldn't get her words out of his head. He tried everything he could think of to forget about Amina and the pregnancy—all of it. But maybe she was right. He needed to do what would be best for his future family, as if to reinforce what his grandmother was trying to tell him.

"Hello, Mr. Holland. The results are in and will be couriered to your office this afternoon," the receptionist said. He thanked her and hung up. Well, now it would be official. He would know very soon whether or not he was a father. As he drove on, he made a decision and called Dru.

"Dru, I want you to draft an agreement for me. I want Amina to sign off all custody of the child to me as the father." Dru asked if he was sure, and he confirmed he was.

"Are you sure that's what you want to do? If she disagrees, we could take her to court, but you have to have a damn good reason why she shouldn't have custody to win that. And custody battles always get messy, trust me on that," Dru said.

True, Kieran was aware that courts tended to favor mothers for custody. But Kieran had two things on his side that Dru wasn't considering, money and access to some damn good lawyers.

"I'm sure," Kieran said before hanging up. His grandmother was right about one thing. He had to do right by his family. Amina couldn't have the baby in that dank and unsafe apartment. What kind of life would that be for a child? What if he or she got sick? Or worse, in that kind of place. Everything about that neighborhood was a walking hazard waiting to happen. He didn't even want to think about the crime that was surely going on. Even beyond that, it was apparent she couldn't afford to look after herself, let alone a child. It would be better for everyone if Kieran took care of things. He could always ask his sisters and grandmother for help, and what they couldn't do, he'd hire someone to take care of it when he was at work.

He arrived at his office and asked Hannah not to let anyone disturb him. Sitting on his desk, mocking him, was a manila folder. The piece of paper that would change his life forever.

He took a deep breath as he opened the manila folder. Uncharacteristically, his hands were shaking. He looked down at the paper, and his chest tightened. She was right. The baby was his.

He paged Hannah immediately.

"I want to speak with Amina. She's the barista with the little stand in the cafeteria," he explained. Send her up to my office immediately," he said. After two minutes, Hannah called him back.

"I'm sorry, sir, but Miss Bethune hasn't been in today," she said. Odd. Anyone who worked in the cafeteria was there from Monday to Friday during business hours. She should have been there today. And he knew it wasn't like Amina to miss work without a good reason. For heaven's sake, he once caught her working at A Cuppa Love with the worst cold he had ever seen.

He called down to internal business affairs to request her file. Once he had her contact information, he tried her cell. It rang endlessly until all he got was her voicemail. With a grunt, he looked at her next of kin contact and tried that—same result, nothing but voicemail.

Now he was worried. It's one thing if she didn't answer her phone, but her sister should have, especially if something was wrong.

Damn it!

Without even thinking, he left the office and drove to her address. He couldn't shake the feeling that there was something horribly wrong. He could not have prepared for what he would find when he got there.

The apartment was completely engulfed in flames. Every instinct he had urged him to run into the inferno and find Amina. He almost barged right past the fire crew outside the building before he spotted Amina sitting outside an ambulance, an oxygen mask on her face. Kieran's legs could have turned to jelly. He felt so relieved. He ran towards the ambulance.

"Are you two alright?" he asked suddenly, breathless. Amina coughed horribly but nodded. Not convinced, he turned to the paramedic.

"They're fine. Just a little smoke inhalation, but due to their health conditions, we're taking them to the hospital to be monitored just to be safe." Amina's eyebrows knitted together. Kieran didn't know what health conditions they were talking about when it came to Serena, but he could tell that the concept of two hospital bills concerned Amina.

"I'll take care of the hospital bill," Kieran whispered. Relief flashed over Amina's eyes.

"I will follow behind the ambulance," he said. Ideally, he

would take them in his car, but he doubted the EMT would let him.

"Where are we going to go?" Amina asked in a tiny, scared voice. Kieran felt a tug in his chest. Although he had dogged their neighborhood and apartment, he knew it was at least something. Now they had absolutely nothing left.

"You're going to move in with me. Both of you," Kieran said with an air of finality. Amina and Serena protested, but he wouldn't hear any of it. He reiterated his sentence, got in his car, and closely followed the ambulance.

CHAPTER 13
Mending Fences

It was amazing how life could continue to surprise Amina. She thought she had already been dealt a more challenging hand than most. But now, with her apartment completely and utterly gone, she had nothing left.

She stared around her room at Kieran's house. The shock of recent events had long worn off, and by this point, she couldn't help but feel numb to the idea of one more bad thing happening. On the plus side, she did have one reason to be grateful. Amina hated to admit it, but it was kind of Kieran to invite Serena and her into his home. Compared to his family's mansion, it was small. However, to Amina and Serena, it was still larger than anywhere they had ever lived. And a little unexpected, to say the least. Still, his home was far more comfortable than their cramped apartment. Even his guest beds were bigger than both Serena's and Amina's.

And he seemed to be warming up to the idea of the baby. Kieran told his entire family about the baby, and they were thrilled. So thrilled that, he had told Amina, they were beginning hope they would get back together.

"Oh... well, that's nice," Amina had said, unsure how to respond when he told her.

"I told them not to get too ahead of themselves; don't worry," he said. Amina should have felt relieved, but at the same time, she couldn't help but feel that familiar disappointment.

But he was proving to be present when it came to the baby. He went with her to every doctor's appointments. He bought many baby clothes and supplies without her even having to ask. However, Kieran ignored Amina when it didn't concern the baby. He would come home from work, eat dinner, and retire to his bedroom.

It was kind of starting to piss her off. She understood if he wanted to care about the kid. She also cared about the baby. But she wasn't just his walking incubator. It would be nice if he would at least talk to her cordially. Was that honestly too much to expect?

A knock sounded on the bedroom. Esme poked her head in with a smile.

"I just thought I would come to check to see how you're doing," she said, crossing the room to hug Amina. Amina resisted the urge to groan as she stood up to return the hug. The leggings and tank top she was wearing were far too tight on her at the moment. Amina felt like she was getting bigger and bigger by the minute.

"Oh my. Those look a little... snug," Esme said. Amina felt the heat rush to her cheeks. She knew what she was wearing wasn't exactly flattering, but her little loose clothing was lost in the fire.

"Yeah, I don't have much left from the fire," Amina said sheepishly. Esme gave her an empathetic smile.

"Kieran should have taken you shopping then," she said with a disappointed head shake. Amina bit her tongue. She knew Esme adored Kieran. How would she tell her that her grandson barely looked at her except to ask if she needed more prenatal vitamins?

As if God-sent, Serena came into the room. Amina couldn't help but breathe a sigh of relief. The last thing she wanted to discuss was Kieran and her fat pregnant body.

"I got some maternity clothes from the church charity drive," Serena said, fumbling with a big cardboard box in her arms. She set it down on the bed and pulled the clothes out. Amina forced a smile. They were dated and definitely too baggy, but at least she would be comfortable. Even if she knew she would look like a whale in them.

"What on earth are these?" Esme asked, holding a garish floral print dress with disdain.

"I need maternity clothes, but I can't afford to go shopping right now," Amina said, feeling even more embarrassed. She had debated asking Kieran to get her some maternity clothes, but his indifference to her presence made her bite her tongue. If he didn't care to talk to her about anything other than the baby, why would he care if she was uncomfortable?

"No. Absolutely not," Esme said with an air of finality. She dropped the dress on the bed as if it had bitten her. Then she made her way over to her purse and looked at Amina and Serena expectantly.

"Well, come on then. We're going shopping," she said.

"But Esme, I can't—" Amina tried to protest, but she was cut off by Esme holding her hand up.

"And that is exactly why I'm going to pay for everything. The mother of my grandson's child will not dress in hand-me-down rags or tight, uncomfortable clothing. Now come along. I'm getting old, but even I don't have all day to stop and chit-chat." There was no arguing with her. In a blur, a bewildered Amina and Serena had been rushed into the car. The whole drive, Esme was muttering to herself about needing to have a talk to "straighten that grandson out." Serena looked at Amina with a humorous glint in her eyes.

When Esme said they were going shopping for maternity clothes, Amina hadn't expected to pull up to an expensive-looking boutique. Looking back on the wedding, she really shouldn't have been surprised. The second thing Amina wasn't expecting was that when she walked into the boutique, she was immediately greeted by rows and rows of lingerie.

"Esme, this isn't a maternity store," Amina said slowly, trying to hide how incredulous she was.

"Don't worry, my dear. They sell maternity nighties and slips that will look gorgeous on you," Esme said. "We'll get some other maternity clothes as well, but you should always feel your best no matter what you're wearing." She and Serena got to work, grabbing Amina a handful of different things to try on.

"I bet you feel like a model," Serena said, smiling brightly. Amina felt anything, but as she tried more things on, she felt more and more at ease. Esme knew how to pick something that flattered her current body shape, and she soon forgot how self-conscious she was.

"I do have a confession to make," Esme said, coming back with another nightgown. "I did this hoping to knock some sense into that grandson of mine. You may just be the best thing that ever happened to him. As selfish as that sounds, I was hoping you two could fall in love again."

Amina couldn't hold back anymore. Maybe part of it was the hormones. Maybe part of it was the kindness that Esme was showing her. Maybe it was because of Kieran, and perhaps it might have been a little bit of everything all at once. All Amina knew was that the tears were coming, and there was nothing she could do to stop them.

"Oh, whatever is the matter, my dear?" Esme asked, fumbling through her purse furiously for a tissue. Amina couldn't keep it in. She told Esme everything. She and Kieran had struck that deal, and he paid her to be her date. She expected Esme to be shocked and upset, but was surprised to see her nodding calmly.

"I know my grandson. He's always seen things transactionally. Don't know where he gets it from, but that's his nature," Esme said. Amina hiccupped.

"I'm really sorry, Esme. And well, thank you for the clothes, at any rate," Amina sniffed. Esme patted her hand gently.

"Don't be sorry. I believe you were perfect for my grandson. And these old eyes still work, you know. I can tell he felt something, even if he won't admit it. And he needs a woman like you in his life. Can you help him fall in love?" she asked, taking Amina's hand.

"I don't know if I can." Amina shook her head.

"Don't worry, darling. Leave everything to me," Esme said, reassuring Amina. Amina had no idea what Esme meant, but she couldn't help but feel reassured.

Amina stood in the kitchen in her new nightie. Esme had settled on a pale heather-colored lace set, and Amina had fallen in love with it. Then they took Amina to get her hair done. Amina hadn't been overly crazy about silk pressing her hair, but Esme had been so kind that she couldn't refuse. As they were leaving the salon, Esme leaned in and whispered something to Amina.

"If you know how to make a good gumbo, that will warm up Kieran even more," she said with a conspiratorial wink. Luckily, one of the few things Amina's mom had left behind was an old family recipe for gumbo. She had the whole thing memorized by heart.

She gave the gumbo another stir when she heard the door open. The smell must have enticed Kieran because he poked his head into the kitchen. He looked Amina up and down, a look of surprise on his face.

"Why did you silk-press your hair?" Kieran asked. Amina couldn't resist the urge to let out a snort.

"I'm surprised you even noticed," she said.

Despite everything, Amina had to admit that she was glad he had noticed. It gave her a warm feeling she couldn't quite put her finger on. Maybe it was just her hormones again.

"What's that supposed to mean?" Kieran asked, frowning.

"Oh, come on, Kieran, you're not that dense. This whole time, you've been treating me like an incubator. You barely think of me as a person. I'm just the vessel carrying your baby. That's it," Amina said.

There was a tense moment of silence. Kieran looked down at the floor for a moment and had a regretful expression. He opened his mouth, but he couldn't seem to find the right words. He shut his mouth and looked right at Amina.

"I'm sorry. You do look beautiful," he said.

"Thank you," Amina said. She gestured for him to sit at the table. She began dishing up the gumbo into a bowl for him.

"Just a shame about the hair. I like your curls. They're what made me fall for you," Kieran said.

Amina almost dropped the spoon in surprise. She stood there momentarily, unsure if she was supposed to respond.

All she knew for sure was that she was blushing.

CHAPTER 14
Starlit Passion

After that dinner, she and Kieran began to talk. The more they talked, the easier it became to be around him. Things between the two of them were going well—incredibly well, in fact. Amina tried to think of what it was that changed between them. It couldn't have just been the makeover that Esme sprang for. Maybe it was the speech Amina had given him about feeling like a baby factory, but something was different.

They started going out together and doing things other than shopping for baby items. They took walks and went out to eat. All her resentment for him from the wedding had melted away, especially after she had been brave enough to ask him about Nyra over dinner one night.

"Ugh. She wouldn't let go and leave me alone. I wanted to get away from her, but she kept showing up. I thought if I was nice to her, she'd get bored. Then she asked me for a dance even though I was busy," he explained. Amina couldn't help but feel relieved.

"I thought maybe you preferred being there with her," Amina said.

"Oh God, no. I'm sorry if that's how it looked. Is that part of the reason you left the wedding?" Kieran asked. Amina nodded. They were silent for a moment until Kieran laughed.

"What?" Amina asked.

"If I could have told her to take a hike, I wouldn't have had to look for you for four months. Look, Nyra is pretty, but that's it. She isn't kind or sweet or hardworking... or anything like you," he said. Amina couldn't help but smile. He had been looking for her. He never wanted to be around Nyra. And he was far happier around her than he had been around Nyra.

One day, they were both talking about their families. They were prompted when Esme dropped off even more baby supplies at the house. Kieran had just finished telling Amina how Esme nearly sued his school when they refused to do anything about his sister Joyce being picked on.

"I can really see why you love your grandmother so much. She is a remarkable woman," Amina said, staring at all the baby supplies. She almost wanted to cry. She felt so touched by Esme's continued kindness.

"Yeah. You know, she built everything the Hollands have all by herself. She worked harder than everyone in the family to make sure they had a better life than she did. And she stepped up after... well, after many things went down," Kieran said, trailing off. Amina felt a tug in her chest. Without having to ask, she knew Kieran was talking about his parents. When she was around him, she noticed a pattern: he felt very uncomfortable whenever they were mentioned. She didn't want to pry before Kieran was ready to talk about his parents in his own time. After all, she had a sense she knew what he was talking about.

"My mom died when I was really young. She had many health problems; from what my dad told me, they just worsened over time. And right as I finished high school, Serena and

I lost our dad to a drunk driver," she said. Even now, she wondered what her dad would think of all this. Would he be proud of her or think she was stupid for getting pregnant when she was supposed to care for Serena? And even though she didn't have that many memories of her mom, she would have given everything to have her there as she went through all this.

"I'm very sorry," Kieran said, sympathetically putting his hand on her knee. Amina sniffed and nodded appreciatively.

"In a way, I guess that's why this kid is so important to me. I want to be part of their life and be the amazing mom I never got to have. I don't want them to go through what Serena and I went through."

"You will; don't worry. I would never let anything come between you and the baby," he said with such conviction that Amina couldn't help but be a little taken aback. It still surprised her how he never seemed to waver when it came to the baby's welfare. It was like he was made for fatherhood.

"Oh, before I forget, my grandmother wanted me to give this to you," Kieran said, handing her an envelope with a vibrant red wax seal.

"What's this?" Amina asked delicately, taking the envelope in her hand.

"My grandmother thought hosting a charity ball for her sixtieth birthday would be good. In her words, she's 'had enough damn birthday presents,' and now she wants to give back." Amina smiled and accepted the invitation.

The day of the charity ball came, and Amina and Serena were surprised that Scout came storming into Kieran's house with Bristol trailing behind her.

"Scout? What brings you here?" Amina asked as Scout hurried in with a woman quickly in tow. Amina recognized her as the stylist who had helped her get ready for the wedding months ago.

"I'm here to help you get ready for the ball, of course. Consider Bristol and me your fairy godmothers," Scout said. Scout turned to Bristol. "I want romance, mystique, and drama, Bristol," Scout instructed. If Amina didn't know better, she would say the entire Holland family's love language was gifting free makeovers. She remembered the first makeover Kieran scheduled when they were going to Scout's wedding. How nervous and uncertain she had been to even around him.

Now she was not only pregnant with his child, but she was also going to another family event. Maybe all her insecurities at the wedding had been in her head. She thought about the time she wasted that could have been spent getting to know Kieran better had she not run away that night and trusted her gut that there was something between them.

Scout grabbed a gown bag from her stylist and laid it on the bed.

"I can't wait to see my brother's face after we're done with you," she said, her smile illuminating.

Kieran waited anxiously at the door. When Scout said she wanted to help Amina get ready, he knew it would take a while. But the longer he waited, the more anxious he became. After all, it was at a soiree like this that everything went wrong the last time. He hoped that he could show Amina how much she meant to him this time.

He couldn't believe that all of this could have been avoided if he had just been more attentive to her feelings. If he had, they could have continued to see each other. He usually wasn't that big on seeing girls long-term, but he couldn't get enough of seeing Amina. He realized that when he thought she was out of his life for good. Now she was back, and he would do everything he could to improve.

He saw Scout arrive first and saw her beaming at him.

"Wait until you see my handiwork," Scout said proudly. Kieran looked past her and felt like all the air had been sucked from his lungs.

Amina was stunning. The navy-blue dress cinched in at her waist and dropped elegantly to the floor. The skirt fanned out with a dramatic look that drew great attention to her waist. With the sparkling fabric and the ballroom lights, it looked as though she was starlight incarnate.

"You look amazing," he said breathlessly. She bit her lip shyly.

"Thank you," she said. Taking her arm in his, he led her into the dance hall. He hadn't felt this giddy about dancing since his high school days. His grandmother caught his eye and waved him over.

"Be right back," he said to Amina. She smiled and nodded. When he got to where his grandmother sat, she smiled at him.

"Make this one count," she said with a grin. He had no idea what she was talking about and turned to look for Amina. Apparently, he wasn't the only one who thought Amina looked exceptional. As he took his eyes off her for even a moment, two gentlemen swooped in on her. The conversation didn't look predatory, but something about how they were smiling at Amina made his blood boil. He walked over to them and looked them in the eye as he put his arms around Amina.

"Everything alright, darling?" he asked, looking down at Amina with a smile. Not even for a second did he take his eyes off the men. They got the message pretty loud and clear and scampered off. Kieran suppressed a chuckle.

The music changed to a slow dance, and he held out his hand to Amina.

"Shall we?" he said. Amina looked around the room, a flash of anxiety in her eyes.

"I'm afraid to dance. I've never been to a party like this. I'll look so out of place," she whispered to Kieran. He grinned down at her. She bit her lip and glanced nervously back at the dance floor.

"Trust me; you are the most beautiful woman in this room. Anyone would kill to dance with you." Kieran held out his hand and dipped into a slight bow to further prove his point. "So, on that note, may I have the honor of this dance?"

Amina tentatively took his hand, and he led her out onto the dancefloor. From the corner of his eye, he could see Scout flashing him a thumbs-up and tittering at their sisters. His grandmother, from her chair, looked at the two of them with a smile and raised her wine glass, a small show of support.

He twirled her around the room, and it was very easy to forget that anyone else was there with them. At that moment, he only had eyes on her. They danced for hours before Amina indicated she needed to sit down and catch her breath.

"I definitely can't dance like I used to," Amina said, huffing slightly.

"Why don't we call it a night then," Kieran said, taking her arm once more. He glanced back at his grandmother, who gave an approving nod.

When they returned to the house, Amina gave him a flirtatious look.

"I'm going to need help getting out of the dress," Amina said.

Kieran studied her face to see if he was reading the situation correctly. When he saw that there was no hesitation in her eyes, he gently kissed her neck while carefully unlacing the corset backing. It took some effort to disentangle her, but soon the gown sat unceremoniously on the floor.

He cupped her face gently and kissed her. The heat and

passion of the evening came to a peak as the two held each other, kisses roving to all the tender and enticing places that sent shivers up Kieran's spine. When he cupped her breast, Amina moaned, and Kieran couldn't hold back anymore.

He led her to the bed and kissed her breasts and stomach. Then he pulled her against him, feeling the heat of her breath against his skin. His fingers brushed her face as lightly as a feather. With every thrust, he felt closer to her than ever before.

With a shudder and a breathless sigh, the two collapsed onto each other. They lay there in the dark and basked in the gentle blanket of the night.

CHAPTER 15
Together

Kieran looked down at Amina's sleeping form. He had never felt like this in any of his past relationships. Compared to Amina, they all felt so shallow. Maybe it was because he refused to get to know them like he did with her.

Thinking about what would happen if she suddenly disappeared from his life filled him with an ache that jolted him. He didn't want to lose her. He wanted to see her like this every morning and hear the sound of her laughter. He wanted to be there with her for their child's firsts. Even if he thought she couldn't handle it initially, he knew now that parenthood would feel empty and incomplete if he didn't have her there with him.

What had she done to him exactly? One minute, he walked into a cafe, spotted a cute girl, and returned because her smile was pretty and her Cortados were to die for. The next thing he knew, he didn't want to see her leave him. Not now or ever.

Amina stirred beside him and sat up. Kieran felt his heart skip for a brief moment. She groaned and held up a finger.

"Hang on. I'll be right back," she said. Waddling away from him, he heard her stumble into the bathroom and empty the contents of her stomach.

"Sorry," she groaned as she plopped back into the bed.

"Don't be. But should you still be throwing up at this point?" he said as he pulled her closer. He didn't know much about pregnancy apart from the basics, but he had to admit he was concerned. Did having sex somehow make her sick? Or hurt the baby?

"Doc says that while not as common, many women get morning sickness for months into their pregnancy. It's getting better, but I think my body just doesn't like how late I was up last night," she explained as she nestled into his arms. He rubbed her shoulder to offer comfort, and she sighed contentedly.

"Good then," he said. Even this somehow felt odd to him. Cuddling, Amina felt a different kind of euphoria from the sex they had last night. His heart thumped so loudly that he was almost certain Amina could hear or feel it against her back.

"Are you ok? You're being pretty quiet," Amina said suddenly. Kieran debated lying for a moment. That he was ok and there was nothing to worry about. But the truth was, if he didn't express his feelings, he would explode.

Ok, no more bottling it up. If he didn't take a chance right now and lay everything bare to Amina, he just knew he would regret it one day. Maybe it wasn't going to go the way he wanted it to, but he had to take that risk.

"I'm not good at the whole commitment thing," Kieran said. He felt Amina's eyes boring into him.

"Are you about to tell me after everything that this is it?" she asked, an edge of hurt in her tone. He shook his head furiously and gently took her hands in his own.

"Not at all. Just, please let me explain, ok?" he begged. Amina visibly dropped the tension in her shoulders. Kieran could finally sigh in relief. He tightened his grip on her hand. This was going to be a lot harder than he thought.

"My mom cheated on my dad a lot. She either wasn't very good at hiding it or didn't really care to. Dad caught her a few times. I don't remember many details, but the fighting got pretty bad. They could have divorced, but they never did. So Dad did the only thing he could live with, I guess. He started drinking and..." Kieran gulped.

He hadn't expected talking about this to be so hard. He spent years deliberately repressing his childhood memories, but at the same time, it felt like a great weight was slowly being chipped from his shoulders. At any moment, he would finally be able to breathe again, as long as the one he was sharing this with was Amina.

"So Dad wound up drinking a lot. Every time she cheated, it got worse. Grandma and I found him one morning. He died sometime in the night from alcohol poisoning. After that, Mom packed her bags and ran off with one of her boyfriends," he continued. There was a pause for a moment as Amina soaked in his words. A glimmer of sympathy echoed in her dark brown eyes.

"I'm sorry to hear that. That must have been... very hard to deal with," Amina said, squeezing his hand. A wave of emotion flooded through Kieran, and he had to take a breath. As much as he needed to have this conversation, the last thing he needed was to break down. But something about Amina's hand on his was giving him the reassurance and strength that he needed. When he felt he was ready, he continued.

"When I got older, I don't know. I guess I got afraid of relationships because I was worried about being another version of my parents. So, if I got too close to a girl, I would push her away," he said.

There is something here between us. I would be a fool to say there isn't," Kieran said, carefully choosing his words.

"I'm open to exploring whatever we have between us."

"Look, I have feelings for you too. But it isn't just the two of us in the mix right now. I need to know if you want to be part of the baby's life. Even if things don't work out with us, I don't want it to get in the way of parenting. So I need to know if you're in or out regarding that as well," Amina said.

"I know. And I promise to be there for the baby. Even if things don't quite work out with us, I want to be there to support the two of you," Kieran said.

He wondered if he should have mentioned the legal agreement he had drafted. He knew he had to bring it up at some point, but now didn't feel like the right time.

"So then, are you willing to try this?" he asked, feeling his heart leap from his chest to his throat. Amina smiled and pressed a kiss to his cheek.

"Yes, I am," she whispered into his ear.

Now that they had figured things out, everything was going perfectly. However, Amina could tell how uncomfortable Kieran got when his sisters got a little too excited about the concept of their hypothetical future marriage. It honestly made Amina a little awkward, but at the same time, she couldn't help but smirk a little when they did. Kieran had proven himself to be a good guy. She couldn't help but feel a glimmer of excitement at what would come next.

Even Serena was happy for the two of them. She was planning to find her own apartment, though Kieran and Amina had insisted that she could stay with them for as long as she needed to.

"I know, but I want to give you guys as much space as I can. You've got a baby on the way, and I wouldn't want to get in the way," Serena had said. "I'm looking into getting an online certificate or degree or something and seeing what work-from-home options are available. You took care of me longer than you should have, Amina. Let me do this for you, ok?" Amina cried and held her sister for a long time after that.

It was a piece of paper. From what Amina could tell, it looked like it was professionally drafted. She was going to put it back in the folder, but the first sentence caught her eye. Once she saw it, she couldn't tear her eyes away.

I, Amina Bethune, being of sound mind, agree to give custody of my child to the father, Kieran Holland.

She couldn't believe what she was reading. Kieran was going to ask her to give up custody of her baby? Had he been playing her this whole time, trying to sweet-talk her into agreeing? Did he trick her again into falling for him and trusting him?

It felt as if her whole world was closing in on her. Amina needed answers now! She stormed up to him, her heart pounding. Without saying a word, she slammed the paper into his chest.

"What is this?" she asked, her voice terse and harsh. Kieran took the paper from her hand and looked at it. As soon as he saw what it was, he immediately balked and turned pale.

"Where did you find that?" he asked.

"Never mind that. Answer. The. Question!" Amina demanded.

Kieran was silent for a moment before he sighed and looked at her regretfully.

"Before you lost your apartment, I was going to ask you to give me sole custody."

Amina shook violently. She snatched the paper from his hands and tore it before him.

"Do you think I'm some kind of idiot?" Amina asked, her voice brimming over with fury.

"Ok, things may have started out that way; I'll admit that.

But I would never ever tear our child away from you. Not after everything we've been through together," Kieran said.

Amina looked at him. His face held no signs of deception, but still, it didn't explain why.

"Why would you do this?"

"I didn't think you could take care of the baby. Not with where you were living. But then everything changed when you came to live here. I fell for you all over again and never wanted to let you go. I want to do this with you."

"I can't believe this," she said, shaking her head.

She didn't want to believe it. Tears flowed down her cheeks, and she couldn't make them stop.

"I promise I don't feel the same way anymore."

Kieran said as he pulled her into his chest.

"How do I know I can trust you?" she said, her voice slightly muffled against his firm chest.

He pulled away and looked her right in the eyes. "Remember what I said about my parents. I don't want to be them. I want to love you and our baby and cherish every single second together."

She looked up at him. This was the man who had hurt her twice now. But this man also gave her a bigger family than she could have ever hoped for. The man who stepped up when he found out he was a father. She knew he meant what he said.

"Lie to me again, and I'll kill you," she said, pulling him in for a hug. He chuckled.

He chuckled, then kissed her forehead. "Wouldn't dream of it."

CHAPTER 16
A Future with You

Several Months Later

Another contraction rocked Amina's body, and she let out a whine of discomfort. Kieran gripped Amina's hand tightly, reassuring her through the pain. She wasn't sure she could do this if he hadn't been there. Everything hurt, and she wanted to push the dang baby out.

"Just keep breathing, Amina," the doctor said. "You're doing great." She didn't feel like she was doing great. Amina had been at this for four hours now. According to the doctor, everything was progressing rapidly, but she felt it was taking an eternity. But soon, with a final push and a cry, he was there.

Breathless and sweating, Amina stared down at her baby boy. She couldn't believe that he was finally here. It felt like the rest of the pregnancy had passed in the blink of an eye. Of course, that was partly due to Kieran being involved with the whole process.

"What are we going to call him?" Kieran asked, the corners of his eyes moist from tears. Amina stared down at their son, feeling a sense of warmth and love she had never experienced before.

"How about Ellis?"

It was a risky choice. Ellis was the name of Kieran's father. She had been debating it for months but wasn't sure how Kieran would react. But as she glanced back up at him, she saw that he was smiling.

"I guess that makes sense. This way, it's kind of like I'm forgiving him a little. Like a part of me is honoring him and letting him go as a negative influence over my life. Now, I just have this positive piece of my father instead."

Amina couldn't find fault with that logic. She smiled down at their sleeping son.

"Hi, Ellis," she said, the wave of emotions tightening her throat slightly. "Welcome home."

Soon after nursing, Amina was finally allowed to rest as Kieran and the nurses cared for baby Ellis. She slept, but not that deeply. It felt like she had blinked, and then she was wide awake again. She groaned and opened her eyes. She could hear Ellis lightly breathing in the cot next to her bed. She clumsily sat up, still sore.

"Good morning, beautiful," Kieran said, kissing her forehead.

"Look at him. He's perfect," she said as her vision slowly cleared. The blurry figure before her took shape, and she gasped as she fully saw Kieran down on one knee with a ring box in his hand.

Her heart fluttered with shock and happiness, unsure of what was happening but feeling a rush of emotions nonetheless.

"I know that we didn't have the most conventional start to our relationship. But I want us to be a family in every sense of the word. So, Amina Bethune, will you do me the extreme honor of marrying me?" Kieran asked.

"Yes!" Amina squealed, kissing him. He slid the ring on her finger and kissed her again.

﹩﹏﹏﹏﹏﹩

Sometime later.

Amina and Kieran sat at the table with Ellis in their laps, and wedding magazines laid out. They decided they wanted to get married shortly after Ellis turned one. As Kieran pointed out potential boutiques for dresses and talked excitedly about venues, Amina couldn't help but think back to how they had met. All this happiness was because of a deal she made with a billionaire. She had done it to save a life and never expected to gain much more.

And she wouldn't have traded it for anything.

﹩﹏﹏﹏﹏﹩

Ready for a knockout romance? Dive into the world of Skye and Jordan as they fight for love and redemption. Click **HERE** to start **Training the Billionaire** and witness the sparks fly!

START THE PREVIEW!

CHAPTER 1
To Relive a Dream

Little beads of perspiration gleamed off Jordan Turner's well-defined arms. He threw a few jab-right crosses and then jab-cross-left uppercut-cross shadow boxing combinations. His upper body was relaxed, his spine straight but well-controlled as he moved his feet nimbly across the mat. His six-foot-three frame moved effortlessly while he made sure the filming cameras got in the shots of the gear and championship fight he was promoting.

"That's a wrap," the young video producer told his small team that had joined him at Jordan's home training gym.

"Thank you once again, Mr. Turner, for allowing us to film this in your gym." The young producer smiled, a little star-struck. Jordan Turner was a legend in the boxing world. "My younger brother is a boxer and has always been inspired by your career."

"It is always nice to hear that I can still inspire the youth of today." Jordan laughed, taking a sip of water.

"May I ask why you quit, especially when you were at the top of your game, unbeaten?" the young man asked Jordan.

A shadow came across his eyes. "I was at the age where I felt it was time for a change," Jordan said, wiping his damp body and arms with a fluffy blue towel. "To be honest, I have had the itch to return to competing for the past couple of months."

"Oh, wow," the young man said, beaming with delight, "that would be awesome; your fans would go nuts."

"Or they would think I was having an early mid-life crisis!" Jordan laughed, running the towel through his damp hair again.

"I know you probably get this all the time," the young man said sheepishly, "but it would mean the world to my brother if he could meet you."

"Sure." Jordan smiled. "No problem. On your way out, ask Quinton, my agent, for my card."

"That is so great," his young face glowed with excitement, "I can't wait to tell my brother." He walked off to go gather up the camera crew and check the equipment.

"They will check the footage and come back to you for the final review," Quinton informed Jordan after letting the camera crew out. "I had an interesting conversation with the young editor," he continued, raising an eyebrow at his client, who also happened to be one of his oldest friends. "He tells me you are thinking about getting back into boxing."

"He told you that?" Jordan walked through the gym into the shower room. "Or did you overhear that while skulking around in the shadows?" He laughed and threw his dirty towel at Quinton.

"Fine." Quinton fought off the disgusting towel. "I overheard the two of you talking, and the young man was eager to know if it were true. Well?"

"To be honest," Jordan began, as he sat down on the bench to untie the laces of his boxing boots, "I have been thinking about it more and more."

"Come on, Jordan," Quinton leaned back against a locker, "we have been over this. You left the boxing world at the top of your game. Why risk your reputation now?"

"That's the thing, Quint," Jordan pulled off his boots, tossing them into the shoe basket, "I think I got out too early. I feel like I never really got to prove myself or go as far as I wanted to go."

"But look at all you have accomplished since you retired from boxing," Quinton told him. "You are still one of the top male sports models, and let's face it, at thirty, that is a huge compliment."

"Gosh, thanks," Jordan replied, his brow furrowed, "but I think most of the sports companies come to me to ensure I don't start producing my own line of their specialized goods."

"Maybe," Quinton laughed, and then he nimbly dodged a friendly punch thrown at him. "You are still boxing's darling pretty boy." He patted Jordan on the back, instantly regretting it when his hand came into contact with Jordan's sweat-soaked shirt.

"You know I have one more belt to add to my wall," said Jordan, as he pictured his trophy room.

"Why?" Quinton shook his head, "You already hold three of the four major championship belts, which is an incredible achievement."

"I feel there is still a lot more for me to accomplish." Jordan sighed and continued, "I thought the boxing light burned out for me the night Wayne died. But I think I was fooling myself as the light only dulled." His voice dropped to almost a whisper.

"You have to stop beating yourself up about your brother's death," Quinton told Jordan. "Getting over a loved one's death never leaves us; it is always there, but then so are they. We carry them with us in our memories."

"Wow. That's rather deep. Even for you!" Jordan laughed as a telltale red stained Quinton's cheeks.

"Yeah, I lost someone recently, so I know." Quinton gave Jordan a tight smile. "I may not have been that close to my father as I would have liked, but the fact remains, he was still my father."

"I know, buddy," said Jordan, giving Quinton's arm a pat. "It's hard not to think of being able to pick up the phone to call them or not find a message from them."

"Although I never got those from my dad." Quinton smiled; sadly, ", there was always the possibility of getting one while he was still alive. Now, well, I never will, and if I did, well, I would be the first one looking for a priest."

The two men looked at each other and burst into laughter.

"Well, I am going to leave you to clean up because you stink, man," Quinton said, wrinkling his nose. "And I tell you this as your best friend." He ducked as a dirty sock was hurtled at his head as he left the locker room.

———

"Okay," Quinton said as he leaned back into the comfortable sofa, a slice of pizza in his hand. "So tell me again, why are you hell-bent on this stupid idea of getting back in the ring?"

"I told you," Jordan shrugged, ignoring the tantalizing smell of the pizza sitting on his glass coffee table. "I feel like I have more to accomplish."

"You know I think you are completely crazy, right?" Quinton said, biting into his pizza slice. "But I get it. Although I must say, you are rather out of shape for a boxer," he added, glancing at Jordan's midsection. Quinton grinned as he munched on his food, nearly choking when the thrown sofa pillow met his face.

"I realize that." Jordan gave in to the pizza temptation. "The last woman I was with told me the same thing."

"What, that you were losing your mind?" Quinton laughed, getting another whack with a pillow.

"Out of shape." Jordan eyed the gooey mess he was about to take a bite of. "Something about me being in the beginning of a dad's bod." He thought about not eating the slice in his hand, shrugged, and took a bite anyway.

"If this is what you're set on, you know you're going to need a trainer," Quinton told him.

"I want the best. I *need* the best, and old Vic passed away a few years ago," Jordan replied.

"I heard." Quinton watched him. "So unless you have an Ouija board, he's no longer available."

"I know. It was a shock," said Jordan as he took another bite of his pizza. "He was a good man."

"That he was," Quinton replied, agreeing with Jordan. "He certainly boosted your career in a major way," Quinton felt no guilt in taking another slice of pizza.

"I know of a few trainers out there who may be interested in helping you revive your boxing career," Quinton told Jordan. "Having you as a client would be a feather in their hat. I can give them a call in the morning while I work on some tournaments for you."

"Thanks, but keep working on the tournaments," Jordan wiped his hands on a napkin. "I already have a trainer in mind."

"Oh?" Quinton stopped mid-pizza bite, his eyebrows raised questioningly.

About the Author

Rose M. Cooper read her first novel when she was eight years old. Since then, she has read tens of novels and twice as many short stories. She, however, did not discover her special knack for writing romance fiction until a decade later.

Now a full-time author with a specialty in contemporary romance, Cooper writes sensual yet relatable love stories designed to hook her readers at first glance. She views writing as another outlet to creativity, and thus has no intentions of setting down her pen just yet. There are many intriguing love stories to be told, and Cooper is set to tell them all.

She hails from New York and currently makes her home in Copiague, New York with her husband, her black cat and her Maine Coon cat. When she is not writing, you will most certainly find her around computers or getting her nose stuck in a book.

facebook.com/RoseMaeCooper

twitter.com/rosemaecooper

instagram.com/rosemaecooper

tiktok.com/@rosemaecooper

amazon.com/author/rosemaecooper

WANT TO BE FIRST TO KNOW?!

JOIN MY NEWSLETTER!
ROSEMAECOOPER.COM/NEWSLETTER

Did it captivate you? Review!

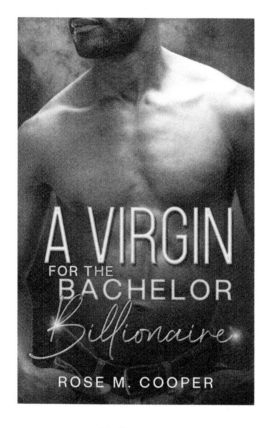

rosemaecooper.com/A_Virgin_for_the_Bachelor_book

Printed in Dunstable, United Kingdom